Shifting Horizons

Stories of lives lived and journeys taken

Sheena Billett

Vanstone Press

For Glen, who inspired me to write

Contents

Acknowledgments

Thanks to Sue, Glen, Sheila and Steve, my best critics and encouragers, to Kostis Pavlou for his stunning cover design, my special colleague, Frances Cooper (fcproof.com) for proofreading and editing these stories, and, finally, to all my readers for keeping me going.

Foreword

I started on these pieces around a year ago when my wife suggested I step out of my editing and proofreading comfort zone and start writing my own stories. As a result, I have been on my own perilous journey into the unknown over the last twelve months! My first piece was *A Question of Life and Death*, and from then on, I was hooked and there was no going back. A number of these stories and pieces of flash fiction have appeared in online magazines and anthologies. Many thanks to *Secret Attic* and all my SA buddies, *Café Lit*, *Glittery Literary*, *The Writer's Club* and *Fiction on the Web*, for giving me the inspiration to keep writing and for giving me the confidence to bring my writing together into this anthology.

I spent some time trying to order this collection and connect stories with similar themes together only to discover that any attempt to marshal my creations into any kind of cohesive order was like herding cats, so I have left them to do their own thing. The only structure is a tenuous path through the seasons to Christmas in my final story. From time to time you will come across flash fiction stories, an increasingly popular genre of short pieces, usually less than 300 words. They are almost a bridge between prose and poetry.

In addition to lives lived and journeys taken, other recurring themes in the collection are: growth, escape and freedom, choices, along with the healing properties of true love, art, music, gardens and trees. You can do a pick and mix or start at the beginning – it's up to you. I hope the stories will make you smile, nod knowingly, gasp, and maybe shed a tear or two, as you travel.

Shifting Horizons

The 'Horizons' theme in this story gave me the idea for the title of this collection, so it comes first.

BETTY ANXIOUSLY STUDIED THE horizon and wondered what might be beyond, tantalisingly just out of sight. She hoped it would be more of the same: Wednesdays, hair dresser; Fridays, choir; Sundays, church. She couldn't imagine things being different any time soon other than an inevitable visit to the dentist, and maybe the doctor if this hip didn't start behaving itself soon. Everything was flat calm just as it had been for the last three years since Reg had angrily and resentfully disappeared over his own horizon.

If you asked Betty, she would say that the horizon was probably about two weeks away. She knew there were landmarks beyond, as yet out of sight, but

1

what form those events might take were unknown. Things such as Christmas and the autumn concert with her choir. She turned the page on her calendar and October was reassuringly blank. Betty didn't want any storm clouds gathering in the distance to disrupt her quiet, ordered life. The long years with Reg had been turbulent and noisy, but Betty had clung on to the wreckage of her marriage because she couldn't imagine any alternative life – better the devil you know, had been her motto.

Today was Wednesday – hairdresser day. Betty put on her raincoat. It had a hood and she didn't want her newly done hair to get wet on the way home. It was looking like rain. She decided against an umbrella – too much to carry, and, picking up her bag and keys, Betty set off for the bus stop.

Much to her consternation, she spotted a hooded youth already ensconced on the bench seat. Betty slowed her pace, wondering for a moment if she should take a detour past the shops and catch the next bus once the hooded person had gone, but that would make her late for her appointment with Carol and she didn't want to be fobbed off with one of the other girls. In any case, Betty prided herself on being punctual.

She arrived at the bus stop and stood as far away from the hoodie as possible. They were engrossed on their phone – no doubt looking at a load of rubbish, Betty thought primly to herself.

A crash made her jump, and she turned as the girl swore. Betty turned to see her bend with some difficulty to try and pick the phone up. She could tell it was a girl now, from her voice and delicate features. As she bent forwards her hoodie fell back to reveal a bald head. Embarrassed, Betty looked away.

'Do you think you could pick my phone up for me? Sorry to bother you.'

Reluctantly, Betty turned and looked at the tears welling in the girl's eyes. She retrieved the mobile and handed it to its owner. 'Thank you so much. I know it's pathetic I can't even pick up my own phone!' And much to Betty's alarm the girl started to cry. She fidgeted uncertainly, wishing the bus would come.

'It's this bloody cancer! The chemo has made my fingers numb, so I keep dropping things and it hurts when I bend. I feel like a bloody old woman.'

Betty decided not to be offended.

The girl's hand flew to her mouth. 'Oh God! I'm so sorry. I didn't mean...'

'It's okay.' Betty sat down beside her.

'I'm Jessie.'

'Betty,' said Betty. For some reason she had abandoned the usual 'Mrs Brown.'

She looked more carefully at Jessie, noting the shadows under her hazel eyes, now red from crying. 'Where are you going?' asked Betty with genuine curiosity. For some reason she needed to know more about this sad girl.

'Off to my next round of chemo. I'm not really supposed to go on the bus, especially not on the way home, but there's no choice, and anyway, I usually get home before the after-effects kick in. Only a few more sessions after this and then I'm in the clear, hopefully.'

'Well you're not going on the bus today, Jessie,' Betty said firmly, all thoughts of the hair appointment forgotten. 'Can you use your phone to call a taxi?'

Jessie lifted her head and met Betty's gaze. 'Are you for real?'

'Indeed I am.'

'Okay, well I have the Uber app – not that I've ever used it much.'

'Can you call a taxi to pick us up here?'

Jessie worked on the phone, intelligent concentration evident in her focused gaze. 'Okay, so I need to put some bank details in for the payment – it's all done online with Uber.' Betty felt a twinge of panic at giving her card details to the internet, but it felt important to help this girl, and she berated herself for her earlier thoughts that all young people in hoodies were bad. Didn't everyone wear them these days?

Jessie tapped in the details from Betty's card and sat back. 'They'll be here in two minutes. Look, there he is.' Jessie handed Betty the phone, and she held it gingerly, afraid that the picture would disappear from the screen. She saw the flashing car icon a few streets from where they were, moving steadily towards them.

'Goodness me. Whatever next?'

Jessie looked no further than the end of each day. Today was no different. She got up, drank some strong coffee from the Nespresso machine, checked her head was smoothly shaved, and fixed the now-familiar make-up.

She usually frequented bus stops as that's where lonely old people were often to be found. And often, they were not poor. Today, she had hit the jackpot with Betty – actually harvesting her bank details. But who would have thought that the old woman would then want to come to the hospital with her? Jessie had done her best to shake Betty off, but she was surprisingly tenacious. When they arrived at the hospital, Betty had insisted on booking the driver to take Jessie home after her treatment, and Jessie had to think on her feet to come up with a fake address. She heaved a sigh of relief as she waved from the door of the oncology department, and Betty at last turned and walked away. Jessie fished the phone out of her pocket and retrieved Betty's bank card details with swift efficiency. She probably had about twenty-four hours before the fraud would be spotted and reported. Old people didn't usually do online banking, but the bank would alert Betty by phone before the day was out, and Betty was probably the sort of person who still answered calls on her landline.

At the library, Jessie was soon hard at work on the computer. Amazon was her one-stop shop for most things, and today she was shopping for books for her Open University course, and maybe she would treat herself to some new clothes, and a different wig. It was time for a new hairstyle. The most important and expensive thing she left until last; paying this term's tuition fees. Jessie held her breath as she typed in the card details – she had made sure to get Betty's address, saying it was necessary for the Uber account. Reassured by the confident *Thank-you for your payment* message, Jessie promptly shut down the computer.

Betty never made it to the hairdresser. Having left Jessie at the hospital, she had got a bus home. Now she was sitting in the conservatory with a cup of tea, thinking about Jessie and feeling increasingly anxious. She got out an old A-Z and looked up the address Jessie had given to Uber – and as she suspected, it didn't exist.

A phone call to the bank to cancel the card revealed that Jessie – if that was even her name – had wasted no time in spending Betty's money. But it was what she had spent it on that shocked Betty most. Books and a large payment to the Open University of all things! Apart from the annoyance that she had been taken in, the strongest emotion Betty felt was curiosity. What was this girl studying? Why would she go to such lengths to get an education? Somehow this was not the type of young person Betty had imagined would con you out of your money.

Awake until the early hours of Thursday morning, Betty decided to do some detective work, but there were several hours until she could make any enquiries so she drank several cups of tea and made a list of all the ways she could possibly track Jessie down. Suddenly the horizon had become very close – only a few hours away, at 9 o'clock, but it crept forwards at a snail's pace as Betty waited.

A few minutes after nine – she should probably give the OU people time to take their coats off – Betty rang the Open University, having got the number from Directory Enquiries. A rather brusque, no-nonsense voice answered the call and Betty was reminded of her old French teacher. Having explained her dilemma and the fact that she wanted to find Jessie to get to know her, rather than get retribution, Betty was faced with the brick wall of identity protection.

'Even though she stole my money, she still has the right to protection?' Betty was tapping her foot in irritation.

'I'm afraid so. Whatever any of our students do outside of the university, does not allow us to divulge such information.'

'Even though I want to help her?' Betty found herself saying.

'I'm afraid so.'

'Well, thank you anyway.' Polite as ever, Betty huffed and replaced the receiver. This was a serious set-back. She consulted her list. The next possibility was to hope to meet Jessie at the bus stop again, but after a few days of walking up and down the road and loitering around the shelter, Betty felt that this was more than her hip could take.

Back to the list. The next option was to visit other places where she imagined Jessie might go, such as the library, or fast-food outlets. At the library Betty was happy to spend hours whiling away the time; she could take out membership and even start reading again, something she used to do voraciously when she was young. Fast-food outlets, however, were another thing altogether and Betty was out of her comfort zone, having never been inside a MacDonald's or Burger King.

She steeled herself to make a visit and found herself at the counter in the MacDonald's on the high street, overwhelmed by the number of options available to her.

'What would you recommend for someone who has never had MacDonald's before?' she asked the server, a young girl with a long ponytail pulled through the hole in her baseball cap.

'You've never eaten McDonald's?' Anna, said shaking her ponytail in disbelief. 'Wow! That's a first for me – a MacDonald's virgin!'

'Well, I wouldn't put it quite like that,' Betty clutched her bag to her chest and frowned.

'Okay, we-ell,' Anna drew out the vowel as she looked at Betty appraisingly. 'What about a Big Mac and a side of fries?' she suggested, blissfully unaware of Betty's discomfort.

'Yes, I'll have that,' said Betty decisively.

A few minutes later she was at a plastic table with a huge paper cup full to the brim with weak tea and her MacDonald's. Betty bit into the burger gingerly and was pleasantly surprised. Before she knew it, she'd eaten the whole meal.

After a few weeks of detective work, Betty discovered that each day could be different. She found a whole new world of horizons in the books she read at the library, so much so that Jessie could have come and gone without Betty even noticing. But somehow, it didn't matter. At the moment she was working her way through Daphne du Maurier and was even wondering if she might take a little trip to Cornwall.

MacDonald's became a weekly visit. Anna suggested something new from the menu each time, but Betty's favourite was still the Big Mac and fries. One Friday teatime, Betty was tucking in to Filet-o-Fish in a window seat, when to her horror she saw Alan and Cynthia from choir approaching along the pavement. Her first instinct was to turn away from the window and hope they didn't look in, but then something quite remarkable happened. Betty found herself smiling and waving at them, secretly enjoying the shocked faces before they recovered themselves and waved hesitantly back.

Although Betty's horizons were broadening, a few weeks later, she had to admit that the detective work had not been successful. She consulted her list, now tucked behind the clock, and discovered there was only one place left to check – the place she'd last seen Jessie - the hospital.

The next day Betty set off for the hospital, enjoying the unhurried, meandering progress of the bus. She saw parts of the town she had never been to before and made a mental note to revisit once her detective work was over.

At the hospital, Betty followed signs to the oncology department and arriving at the reception desk she hesitated, unsure about her next step.

'Can I help you?'

'I've just come to meet someone from the chemotherapy suite,' improvised Betty, noticing the sign from the corner of her eye.

'Can you give me a name?' The receptionist looked at Betty over the top of her glasses.

'Mine, or the person I'm meeting?' Betty was desperately playing for time. Suddenly this visit seemed very important.

'Both. If you give me your name, I can give them a message that you're waiting.'

Betty swallowed. 'Jessie.'

'Oh, Jessie! She shouldn't be much longer. And you are...?'

'Betty...'

'I'll let them know,' she said rising from her seat.

Betty sat with her bag on her lap, her mind racing. Could this really be her Jessie? Unlikely, she thought. But what were the chances of someone else called Jessie being here?

The receptionist bustled back to her desk. 'Only a few minutes, they're just getting her meds ready.'

Betty nodded and clutched her bag tightly.

The minutes ticked by, the waiting almost too much to bear. But it felt more important than ever now.

The doors opened and there was Jessie. Betty recognised her at once, although this time she had hair.

Jessie regarded her with undisguised hostility. 'What're you doing here?'

'Looking for you,' Betty said, suddenly calm.

Jessie's eyes darted from side to side as if she was looking for some escape.

'It's okay. I just want to talk to you.' Betty gave a sly glance at the receptionist who seemed to be intent on something on her screen. 'Even though you stole my money.' Betty noted the imperceptible flicker of the receptionist's eyes and enjoyed the moment.

'Are you okay to have a coffee, or do you need to get home? We could call you an Uber.'

'Are you fuckin'with me?' Jessie's knuckles were white as she clung onto the back of one of the orange, plastic waiting chairs.

A few minutes later they were in the hospital cafe. 'I've been trying to find you, because I want to know what you're studying, whether you really do have cancer, and why you've suddenly got hair.'

'Okay.' Jessie sighed and folded her arms on the table. 'It's no fun having cancer and chemotherapy, so I thought I might as well make the most of a bad job. I'm studying psychotherapy, and I don't have hair, this is a wig.' She leant back as though waiting for a reaction.

Betty smiled through widened eyes. You're training to be a *psychotherapist*?

'Yup! That took the wind out of your sails, didn't it?

'But why?'

'Why not? Knowing what makes people tick can be a useful skill. To say nothing of learning how to get people to trust you.'

Betty regarded Jessie in silence, aware that she was looking prim, and knowing she was exactly the sort of person Jessie despised.

'What? You disapprove of what I've spent your money on?'

'I wouldn't say that, exactly, but why not train in order to help people rather than take advantage of them? Isn't that what psychotherapy is supposed to be about?'

'Maybe in your world, but not in mine,' Jessie hissed.

'Well, anyway, I've been looking for you because I want to help. Anyone who is as ingenious as you in funding their university education deserves a leg-up in my book.'

'Oh, and don't forget the cancer pity card while you're at it.'

Had Betty detected a hint of something softer behind Jessie's harsh words?

'How about we start by continuing with the Uber rides to and from your chemotherapy sessions – above-board this time?'

Jessie was exhausted in spite of the Uber ride home. She was nearly at the end of her treatment and the long haul of chemo was taking its toll. Drinking some flavoured water – she couldn't face coffee any more – Jessie thought about Betty. She wondered if the shock had registered on her face when Linda from reception told her someone called Betty was waiting for her. Betty? *That Betty?*

There was only one exit from the suite so Jessie couldn't avoid her victim. She could have told Linda she didn't want to see her, but deep inside there was a curiosity to know why Betty was there. How had she known where to find her? And anyway, she couldn't very well attack Jessie with her handbag, or her tongue, in full view of Linda – after all she was a cancer patient.

The conversation in the hospital cafe had annoyed and intrigued Jessie in equal measure. Her first instinct was to classify Betty in her Middle-Class Do-Gooder file. But she wasn't picky, Jessie would take any help she could get to reach her goal of getting a degree. A goal that, even now, still seemed way, way beyond the horizon. Jessie lived one day at a time; she didn't look far ahead, other than her hospital appointments which peppered the calendar in her phone for weeks to come. Each day was about survival – taking her meds, conning old people into buying her food, and on good days, working on her OU course.

Jessie knew that education was her passport out of the life she found herself in, and she'd always been fascinated by people – why they did what they did, and what they were thinking. She knew she'd lain it on a bit thick with Betty about the whole

'I'm learning how to con people' line, but something told her that Betty had seen though the façade of bitterness and callousness.

Two years later...

Betty studied the young woman sitting opposite her in the beach-front cafe. Jessie was studying the menu with the same look of concentration she'd worn at the bus stop so long ago. Had it really only been a couple of years?

'How did the check-up and scans go?'

'Still all cancer-free, so I'm celebrating!'

'And the interview?'

'Are you ever going to stop being my mother?' Jessie rolled her eyes. 'Good. I got the job, so double celebration. Just as well the NHS is desperate for psychotherapists at the moment.'

Betty reached across the table and took Jessie's hand. 'I'm so glad, Jessie. I knew you could do it!'

'Thank you for believing in me, Betty.' Betty revelled in the shared affection and respect of the fleeting moment. 'And what about you, gallivanting around the world with your new hip?'

'Well, I'm not going back to China, and I loved South America, but I think my absolute favourite is Italy. I've started an online Italian course – those computer lessons at the library have really paid off. I still go there every week, to read. Somehow it makes reading more special. At the moment I'm working through E.M. Forster.'

'Wow! There's no stopping Mrs Brown now!' Jessie gave Betty's arm a playful prod.

'What do you think about a little Italian holiday sometime? I could practice my new language skills on you.'

'Yes, but who'll be paying?' Betty saw the twinkle in Jessie's eye.

'We-ell, how about I give you my credit cards details and you pay?'

They chinked their coffee cups together in agreement, neither of them worrying too much about horizons. They were too busy enjoying the moment.

Originally published on https://cafelit.co.uk/ 10 February 2022

Never on a Saturday

IT WAS A SATURDAY, I remember because I went always went shopping on Saturdays with my friend, Mia. We would have lunch out and then browse around the shops, or maybe see a film. Those were the days when I was teaching, and Saturday was a brief, luxurious day in my otherwise stressful life. Sundays were for chores, and dread of the looming week ahead.

I came across *Fight for the Life You Want to Live* in the Self-Help section of the book shop. Something drew my fingers to the bright-red cover as if my brain was sending commands without my knowledge or say-so. Then I was reading the back cover, the Contents, and before I knew it I was halfway through the first chapter. It was the sort of shop that encouraged reading and browsing so I bought an obligatory coffee and spent the rest of the afternoon lost in the fight for my life. Mia, huffing in annoyance, went home.

Part of me knew I shouldn't be taken in, and I imagined my no-nonsense sister, Ellie, shaking her head in despair at this 'self-help garbage.' But somehow, I was gripped. Here was a way forward. I bought the book and spent the rest of the weekend immersed in The Fight. I dutifully answered questionnaires, made candid notes about what I hated about my life and what I wanted instead. I sorted out my priorities and planned my escape.

I set off for work on Monday morning full of energy, my letter of resignation – the bomb that would trigger my new life – nestling in my bag. The end was in sight; four more weeks and then I'd be free. I felt light-headed and giddy. My vision, dutifully described in the exercise for Chapter 3, of sitting in a beachside coffee bar, notebook in hand, writing my first novel, was dizzyingly close to coming true. Re-mortgaging the house to raise enough funds for my adventure was completed the following week. I felt as if I was walking on air – way above – looking down on everyone else's hum-drum, boring lives.

Before I knew it, I was sitting by the Mediterranean with a notebook, smugly imagining my former colleagues on break duty in the grey, cold, concrete playground. There was only one problem. My notebook lay, pristine, waiting for me to write my inspired thoughts – of which I had zilch.

As the weeks passed, the glistening sea became exhausting, like a friend who is fun and exciting to be around at first but who eventually becomes too much. The money was draining away faster than I had imagined and I moved from hotels to hostels – hardly conducive to writing. When I only had my air fare home left, I admitted defeat and surrendered.

Now I am struggling to get by with only anti-depressants and benefits to help me through. I can go to the shopping centre any day I want, but I can't face seeing anyone from my old life.

I don't go there on a Saturday.

A Question of Life or Death

HER FINGER HOVERED OVER the email. The answer had come sooner than Anna had expected and she wasn't sure whether she was ready for the message it was bringing. Her gaze shifted to the apple tree now resplendent in full blossom, its annual cycle continuing regardless of the events of her own life – so small in the grand scheme of things she reminded herself, trying to minimise the turmoil that was possibly about to be unleashed. How could a few insignificant words mean so much?

Enough prevaricating. Time for action – to face things head-on as her counsellor advised. Anna read the email.

It was as she expected, her worst fears realised. She read the sparse contents again; the DNA test confirmed that Piers was the father – no mistake! She sat, motionless, the phone in her hand until it rang

...and kept ringing, childlike in its persistence, Anna sighed impatiently and pressed the green icon.

'Well? Come on, spill.'

'Yes, Mum was right.' Anna passed a weary hand over her face.

'Oh my God. what're you going to do?'

'I... I don't know. I thought I was ready for this, but now...'

'Right, I'm coming over.'

'Liv, it's okay, you don't need—'

'I'm on my way.'

Anna dropped the phone onto the table and buried her head in her hands.

She was never going to forgive her mother for this...never.

The first time Anna had mentioned Piers, she should have seen the danger signals; she had expected Lorna to have some issues about her dating an older man, but she hadn't been ready for the dismay that her mother hadn't been able to conceal; the way she had clammed up and changed the subject; and how she hadn't been able to get out of the coffee shop fast enough once they had finished their customary hot chocolates.

At the time, Anna had just mentally shrugged thinking that it was her life and she could date who she wanted.

It wasn't until a few months later, when she realised she was pregnant, that she broached the subject of Piers with Lorna again.

This time, there was no mistaking her mother's dismay and panic as she dropped the glass she was holding, her hands flying upwards to clutch her hair, shaking her head. Anna was alarmed as a strange, whining 'No, no, no!' came from between Lorna's clenched teeth.

'What is it, Mum? What?'

'I should have told you. I never should have let this happen!'

'What!' Anna went to her mother and almost shook her.

Lorna took a deep juddering breath. 'When your dad was away on one of his filming trips, I... I had an affair.'

A terrible, inconceivable thought started to take root in Anna's mind.

'With Piers?'

'Yes'

Anna swallowed. 'When was this?'

'The year you were born.'

The heavy silence lasted for many minutes and Anna felt the shoots of a terrible anger growing in her chest.

'And you didn't think to tell me when you knew I was seeing him?'

'I know...I know I should have, but knowing Piers, I assumed it was just a fling and that he would soon move on. And I thought it was best not to complicate things for you.'

'Complicate things for me? So let's be clear here; you're saying that Piers is my father.'

'Well, he might not be.'

'You don't say!' By now, Anna was pacing restlessly around the room.

'I did have a one-night stand with someone else,' Lorna said, looking at the floor.

'Right, so what am I supposed to do now?' Anna came close and forced Lorna to meet her gaze.

'Maybe a DNA test? Maybe you're not Piers's.'

Suddenly Anna had been overwhelmed by the toxic mixture of emotions swirling in her head and had needed to put some space between herself and her mother. She grabbed her bag and ran out of the house, gunned the engine in her car and just drove.

Later that night, she had finished with Piers, abruptly and ruthlessly, without telling him about the baby.

The slamming of a car door and running footsteps brought her back to the present and the welcome sight of Liv appeared around the side of the house. Liv took Anna in her arms where she cried angry, frightened, despairing tears.

'Okay, time for a drink,' said Liv, gently tucking a strand of hair behind Anna's ear when she was spent. 'Come on, let's go inside.'

Once settled on the settee, each with a glass of chilled wine to hand, Liv looked into Anna's eyes.

'So what next?'

'I've no idea. I think I just kept hoping it wouldn't be true.'

'As I see it you've got three options: one, have the baby and deal with whatever that brings; two, have an abortion – you've still got time; three, tell Piers when it's too late to have a termination, have the baby and make him cough up plenty of money and take responsibility – something he's never had to do before, it seems.'

Anna took the glass of wine and looked at it. 'Well unless I'm going for option two, I'd better not have any more of this.'

'How are you feeling?' Catherine said, her glasses perched on the end of her nose.

'I don't know...such a mixture of things. I'm panicking because I don't know what to do. What do you think I should do, Catherine?'

'You know better than to ask me that,' said Catherine gently.

'Well what's the point of me paying for these sessions if you can't tell me what to do? I've faced things head-on, like you said – so now you're going to leave me in the lurch?'

Catherine regarded her silently for a few minutes, until Anna could stand it no longer.

'I'm done with this! I'll make the payment online later.'

Once again, Anna found herself in her car wanting to drive somewhere...anywhere.

Eventually she stopped for a coffee at a motorway Costa and looked at her phone; there was a message from Catherine:

> *Remember that whatever you decide, this pain will pass and you will cope.*

Anna huffed in irritation and threw the phone onto the seat.

She knew there was another, fourth option, one that she had struggled to not think about. What if she was simply no longer here? Anna knew with a visceral certainty that if she was going to kill her baby she would have to kill herself too – she would not be able to carry on living with that burden. So that was one decision made. The apple tree would carry on blossoming every spring whether she and her baby were here or not, and life would go on.

A family returned to their car from the services, the children clutching pick-and-mix bags. They seemed a perfect, happy family and Anna wondered where they were going, and whether they too had their secrets and burdens, but were good at covering them up...for the children. What if, one day, it might be her and her child doing mundane things like buying sweets at motorway services? Mundane for the adults, maybe, but a highlight for the children. Would she be giving her child small pleasures – sweets for a long journey? She thought about all the wonderful experiences she could share with her child. Could she still give her child a good life in spite of everything? Did she have a right to punish her child for the anger she felt towards her mother and Piers?

She rang Catherine. 'Can we talk? I'm sorry about earlier.'

'Of course. I've had a cancellation for tomorrow morning. Could you manage ten o'clock?

It wasn't the first time that Anna was grateful for her freelance work which meant she could be flexible with her time. And she worked from home...was that significant?

Back in Catherine's consulting room, Anna went through the thoughts she'd had in the car park.

'Well, you're still here, so maybe you have come to a decision after all.' Catherine fixed Anna with another of her intense gazes.

'Maybe, kind of. But what if there is something wrong with the baby? What would I tell him...or her? When would I tell them? What about my mother? What about Piers?' The questions tumbled out.

Anna leant back in the chair and sighed. 'It's all too much!'

Okay, just stop with the questions for now, and focus on the fact that you will have the baby. That's enough for now. You'll have plenty of time to work all these things through when you're ready. One step at a time. I know you were angry that I couldn't tell you what to do, but what I can do is be by your side and support you with whatever you decide.'

Anna leant forward. 'Do you really think I can do this? It all seems so scary.'

'As I said, the thing is to take one step at a time. You've done enough for now, so just rest with that. You don't have to make any other decisions right now.' Catherine smiled. 'You have more courage than you realise.'

Anna sat in her garden looking at the apple tree – still dressed to impress. 'One day my child will be here in this spot, looking up at you. It may not be a big thing for you, but for me it's huge.'

She took a deep breath and let the rest of the afternoon settle around her.

Originally published as *The Answer* in *Glittery Literary Anthology 2* June 2021

March Harsh Decision

SHOULD SHE CARRY ON into the unknown, or should she go back? She might be almost there. Cat Hardy sat as the car idled, the wipers fighting a losing battle against the curtain of March rain battering the windscreen. Visibility was almost nil either way. Was the storm ahead of her – the worst yet to come? Or was it behind her, and would she be heading back to flooded roads and fallen trees?

She looked over her shoulder and smiled at Maisie's face – serene and untroubled in a toddler sleep, oblivious to the world outside. She was glad she'd given her daughter her own family name, along with Ben's. Maisie Hardy-Smith. A girl could go places with a name like that.

Making a snap decision, Cat put the car into gear and headed back on to the road. Crawling along as the visibility allowed. She cursed herself for not charging her phone fully before they left, but they had been in too much of a hurry. There probably wouldn't be any signal out here in the back of beyond, anyway.

A flash of lightning instantly illuminated the road ahead for a moment, and Cat could see a turning coming up. Was this the lane she was looking for? There had been no chance to look for a sign. Cat stopped the car, flung her parka over her head and shoulders, and went to look. She was instantly drenched, and the shock took her breath away. Recovering, she felt her way along the front of the car and mercifully in another flash of lightening saw the sign Lower Mount Cottage. Hastily retreating to safety, Cat sat for a few minutes.

Not having seen her mother for over twenty years, and never having been to this house, Cat had no idea how far down the track it might be. But she had got this far, and there was no other option now but to carry on. She turned and inched her way along, bouncing through puddles and potholes, gasping as a branch lashed the windscreen.

Maisie was beginning to stir, and Cat felt a spasm of panic grip her chest. What did she think she was doing, bringing Maisie away from her familiar, comfortable surroundings into this dark, windswept unknown? She gripped the steering wheel, inching forward with deep breaths.

And then the thrashing branches allowed the tantalising glimpse of a flickering light. Could this be it?

Maisie was wide awake now and starting to wail. Cat threw a few comforting words over her shoulder, all her focus on reaching the ever-growing light. By the time she drew up to the door, Maisie was in full-on meltdown mode. Cat took a moment to close her eyes and take a deep breath. This was it – no turning back.

Leaping into action, she flung on her already sodden coat and raced around the car to extricate Maisie from her seat – wrapping her in her favourite blanket – and ran to the door, banging the knocker with all the energy her pent-up anxiety and stress could muster.

Part of Angela appeared in the thin opening the chain allowed, peering out into the darkness beyond Cat and Maisie as if they were transparent.

'Angela! It's me, Cat..'

Angela's gaze refocused on the bedraggled, wailing family on her doorstep. Cat, too, was wailing like a frightened child, but, unlike Maisie, she was making no sound.

'You'd better come in.' Angela released the chain and allowed a wider frame of light to create a threshold over which Cat stepped, holding Maisie tight. Angela shut the door behind them with a thud and spent a minute or two fumbling with various locks and bolts. Satisfied at last, she turned. Cat had put Maisie down, taken off her coat and was now rifling through her bag for a conciliatory drink and snack.

She went in to the nearest room and sat on a chair, Maisie on her lap, and attempted to soothe her with juice and a biscuit. With Maisie pacified, the quiet of the room became overwhelming after all the noise and turmoil of the last hour. Cat broke the silence. 'Hello, Mum. You were expecting us, weren't you?'

Angela stood uncertainly in the doorway, arms folded, hugging her cardigan around herself.

'The kitchen is more comfortable. Shall we go in there? I'll make a cup of tea.' Cat gathered a protesting Maisie, along with drink and snack, and followed Angela down a long, brown corridor, at the end of which was a surprisingly bright and warm kitchen, with an Aga and large wooden table. She settled herself and Maisie, watching Angela move briskly around, seemingly more at ease in this familiar territory.

'Why are you here?' The question threw Cat for a moment. Why *was* she here?

'I... we had to get away. There was nowhere else...' Cat allowed the words to trail off, uncertain how much to tell.

'So I'm a last resort, then.' The anger took Cat's breath away. She hadn't expected this – weren't mothers supposed to be kind and welcoming to their children? She had had vague notions of a returning prodigal child being swept up in a maternal, all-forgiving embrace, all eyes on the granddaughter she hadn't yet met.

Cat had no answer to break the silence.

Angela put two mugs of tea on the table, along with a packet of digestives, helping herself to two of them and dunking them simultaneously in her tea.

'Okay,' she sighed. 'I get it, you were desperate enough to come here, so it must have been bad, whatever you're running from.' She fixed Cat with a blue-eyed stare that demanded answers. Maisie had fallen asleep and was heavy in Cat's arms; she moved to settle her in an armchair beside the Aga, covering her with a dry blanket from the bottomless bag of toddler resources.

She sat down, took a biscuit, and following Angela's example dunked it in her tea, revelling in the comforting warmth of tea, sugar and wheat. Swallowing,, she turned to face Angela, eye to eye.

'I had to get away from Ben. He was becoming more and more unpredictable.'

'Your husband?' Angela eyed Cat's wedding ring.

'Yes. He's always been a drinker, but now it's getting out of control.' Cat sighed, a catch in her breath. 'Everything seems to be my fault – and more recently – Maisie's fault. I can't have that.'

'So whose fault is it?'

'His own, mostly. The business can't sustain the lifestyle he wants, and he's alienating everyone – staff and customers – with his anger.'

'Do you have money?'

Cat leant back in the chair and dragged her fingers through damp, tangled hair. 'Some. I've always kept my own bank account.'

'Good girl.'

Cat's stomach fluttered at this almost-motherlike comment.

'Right. It's late and we should get some sleep.' Angela stood, leaving Cat to take a few hasty gulps of tea before she followed. 'Maisie... is it?' She looked at her granddaughter dispassionately. 'She'll be alright for a few minutes while I show you your room.'

At the top of a brown staircase, Angela turned right and they arrived in a twin bedroom with lino flooring and a sink in one corner. 'This'll have to do you for now. The bathroom's here.' Angela opened the door to reveal a pink, plastic bathroom suite and more lino flooring. Cat couldn't imagine spending more time in there than was absolutely necessary – especially in the winter or on damp, dark nights such as tonight.

'Thanks...Mum. Cat hesitated over the unfamiliar word. 'We'll be fine in here.'

'The beds are aired – and, yes, I was expecting you.'

They returned to the kitchen where Cat gathered up Maisie, and Angela followed, tutting, with all the toddler paraphernalia.

Angela cooked Maisie a boiled egg for breakfast and made toast soldiers. Maisie's eyes widened in delight at the process of dunking them in the runny yoke, and attacked the meal with relish.

'You used to like that, too,' said Angela, her voice softening. 'I guess we're a family of dunkers.'

Cat laughed aloud, feeling something warm and fuzzy at the use of the word 'family'.

'Did your father ever tell you why I left?' Angela was suddenly serious.

'Not really. He just said that you didn't care about us, and that you wanted to live your own life without...baggage.'

'Well he's not around anymore now, so it's time you heard my story.' Angela took a bite of toast and leant forward, elbows on the table. 'After you were born, I wasn't well. They call it postnatal depression now, but back then I'd never heard of it. All I knew was that I couldn't cope, and the feeling that I was a bad mother just grew and grew until I was convinced that I was a bad person, full stop. There was no one to talk to and no help to be got, so in the end I decided that you would be better off without me, and I went. Better than suicide, I thought.'

Cat flinched at the brutal truth. 'So where did you go?'

'I stayed with some university friends and when that got too much for all of us, I lived rough for a few weeks until I met Marie in the library – it was always warm in there. She lived here and asked me if I would like to come and stay, and help out with chores. One thing led to another and then we were...together.'

Cat gasped. A lesbian mother hadn't been part of her imagining. 'Wow!' was all she could manage.

'I'm well past worrying about what you or other people think,' said Angela leaning back and looking away, a roughness in her voice. 'Anyway, last year Marie died – cancer – and she left me this place.'

'I'm so sorry, Mum.' There was no hesitation this time, and Cat reached for her mother's hand.

'Yes...well. Anyway, Marie's family were none too keen about her leaving Lower Mount Cottage to me and are threatening to drive me out. They are not nice people. I haven't done anything to the place, just in case'

'Was that what you were worried about when I knocked on the door?'

'Yes. I don't know what they'll resort to.'

Cat studied a large, ginger cat that had suddenly appeared on the window sill. After a glance, it ignored her and continued grooming.

'That's Marmaduke. He was Marie's cat. I don't think he's ever forgiven me for moving in, either.'

Cat turned to Angela, drained her tea and put the mug firmly on the table. 'Okay, Mum. You've got me now, and we'll face them together. I'm a lawyer, so I'm sure we can come up with something.'

It was Angela's turn to gasp. She looked at Cat – tears in her eyes. 'I was doing a law degree when I met your father, but I never finished it.'

'A family of dunkers and lawyers, then.'

They shared a cautious smile.

Maisie crashed through the moment, dropping her plastic plate and spoon on the floor, now bored with boiled egg and soldiers.

Cat picked her up and held her. 'Maisie, this is your grandma.'

'Gamma.' Maisie stared at Angela with wide, serious eyes.

Angela met the gaze head-on, studying Maisie for the first time. 'She has a look of my sister, Aggie,' she concluded.

'And of you, Mum. There's no doubting that she's your grand-daughter.'

Then Angela held out her arms, Maisie mirroring the gesture. The threesome hug was spontaneous, warm and tight.

'How about we see what the chickens are up to this morning?' Angela stood, wiping her eyes with the back of her hand.

Maisie squealed in delight.

Cat looked at Marmaduke. 'You don't stand a chance against three Hardy women. I'd quit while you're ahead if I was you.'

Marmaduke replied with a cool stare.

Pay-Back

IT STARTED AS A joke. I wanted to make Harriet pay for what she's done. I've been there for her through thick and thin, always at her side, ready to listen to all her troubles. And how has she repaid me? By meeting some new bloke. Now it's Miles this, and Miles that – it makes me sick, it really does!

It was Elsie's idea: 'Why don't you send her a good, old-fashioned anonymous letter?'

'Are you serious? Who sends letters these days?'

'People who don't want to be traced, that's who.'

'What, with words cut out of magazines and stuff?'

'Yup. I've got magazines galore,' said Elsie, gesturing around at the piles of newspapers, magazines and books in her crowded sitting room.

'You haven't got the guts.' She said with a sneer, when I didn't respond.

Suddenly, I wanted to prove Elsie wrong. But more than that, I wanted to make Harriet feel as bad as she'd made me feel. How dare she just drop me like some old piece of rubbish just because she'd moved on? She owed me!

I really enjoyed thinking of all the nasty, hurtful things I could say. In fact I thought of so many, I couldn't decide which to use.

Eventually, the decision was made, and Elsie and I spent a peaceful and surprisingly enjoyable afternoon cutting and pasting.

That evening, it was suitably dark and rainy when I put on my hoodie and posted my poisoned arrow through Harriet's letterbox.

At work, the next morning, I waited expectantly, ready to comfort – just like old times.

As soon as she arrived, without even taking her coat off, Harriet walked straight up to me, so that we were almost nose to nose. 'Right back at you, Clare!' she snarled, throwing the brown envelope on my desk.

But I'm not going to be deterred. I'm sure Elsie and I will find many more creative ways to get back at her. I know that Harriet will need me again...one day. I'm not letting her go that easily.

A Disaster Waiting to Happen

IAN'S COMMITMENT TO JERRY was total, or so he had thought the day they walked down the aisle together. The plan was to pool their resources and start up a property development business. As Jerry was a builder and Ian a financial adviser, they felt that they couldn't go wrong.

Ian's sister, Diane, had her doubts, however, and had voiced them to Ian several times: 'You've only known Jerry a few months. I know you can't resist all that muscle and those abs, but seriously, what are you doing, Ian? You can't just chuck your career in on a whim!'

'I'm not! I don't want to spend my life working for someone else, I want my own business.'

'But it won't be yours, will it? Only half of it. And you're putting in nearly all the money.'

The conversation had been rushed and in low voices while Jerry was getting drinks at the bar. As he returned with their beers, Ian was all smiles and threw Diane a sideways don't-you-dare-say-anything glance.

A few days after their legal union, Ian and Jerry were at a property auction, eyeing up a dilapidated, terraced house in a run-down part of town. There had been a heated discussion about whether they shouldn't have invested in a better area, but Jerry had won out and Ian hoped he knew what he was doing.

Once the house was theirs, Jerry wasted no time in wielding the sledge hammer. 'Everyone wants open-plan these days – you know – for entertaining.'

'I'm not sure that people in this part of town go in for "entertaining," as such,' said Ian, making quote marks with his fingers.

'You'll see. This area'll become up-market in no time,' shouted Jerry above the noise of falling bricks.

Within a few weeks the innards of the house had been hollowed out, leaving a two-storey shell. Ian had been busy with the architect, drawing up plans for the internal lay-out and a small extension.

'We'll call it a conservatory and then we won't need to worry about planning,' said Jerry as Ian measured out the footprint. Ian thought that he would check this out on the quiet with a friend of his in the planning department – just to be sure. All the materials that they needed to restore the house had been ordered and paid for, but Ian found it difficult to feel Jerry's excitement and enthusiasm.

'You need to get a more positive attitude. You're such a worry-ass, Ian. How about you get on with promoting the house online so that we're ready for a quick sale in a few months?'

They arrived on Monday morning to receive the delivery from the builder's merchant and to ceremonially lay the first brick, but as they drew up in Jerry's van they were aware that a small crowd had gathered at the front of the house and that people were looking up at something. Ian felt a tingle of fear as he followed Jerry's 'What the fuck?' out of the van.

As they approached, a young woman with spiky purple hair detached herself from the group and strode towards them. 'Are you the owners of this shit-storm?'

'What're you talking about? This is going to be the start of a new up-market trend for this area,' replied Jerry, hands on hips. 'I'm doing you all a favour,' he added smugly.

'Right! Okay, well then, well what d'you think is going on up there?'

Jerry followed the woman's pointing finger to see what Ian had already noticed. A large crack had appeared across the front of the house.

Two months, much abuse from the inhabitants of the adjoining properties, and thousands of pounds later, Ian had got to know his husband. He knew, for instance, that Jerry had no idea about managing budgets, and very little grasp of the property market. He knew that while he was lying awake at night, worried sick about the money the house was gobbling up, Jerry could sleep without a care in the world. No such worries kept *him* awake. But Ian also knew that he loved watching Jerry wield a sledgehammer, loved his firm, muscled body – Jerry wasn't afraid of hard work. He got quite antsy if he had to sit around for too long.

Granted, the house had been shored up, and eventually fitted out with a stylish open-plan kitchen complete with bi-folding doors onto a paved back yard. 'The kind of people that buy this aren't going to want to spend their weekends gardening,' Jerry had said with a confidence that sent shivers of worry down Ian's spine.

As Jerry had promised, there was some initial interest from outside the area, but when buyers had visited and noted the overflowing bins, rusting bikes, old settees, and discarded fridges that were the features of their prospective neighbours' front gardens, interest evaporated rapidly.

Even when they lowered the price to barely break-even levels, viewings were few and far between. 'Who's going to want live in a house like this round here?' one viewer commented. 'You'd be a bloody target for all the local dodgy types, thinking you had stuff worth nicking. And where's the grass? Our Tina likes a barbecue in the summer, and you can't have a barbecue without grass.'

Blissfully unaware of looming financial meltdown, Jerry was already planning their next project. 'We'll do another one round here, and gradually the word'll get round that this is an up-and-coming area.'

'It doesn't work like that, Jerry. We can't change the demographic of a whole area on our own! It takes years, and lots of investment. And anyway, we can't start another project until this has sold.'

'Oh come on, Ian. With your contacts you can sort us a loan...surely.'

Another thing Ian had always known about Jerry was that he was very persuasive.

To Ian's relief the house did indeed sell a few weeks later. He had stood firm about not starting another project until the sale had completed, and with much grumbling about wet blankets, Jerry passed the time labouring for his builder mates.

Ian had a much-postponed drink with his sister. If he was honest, he'd not been able to face her I-told-you-so face when things had been on a precipice, but now, with a sale almost completed he felt he could face Diane with some restored pride.

'So, you've got a sale then.' Diane scrutinised him over the rim of her wine glass.

'Yup, it's almost completed. Then we'll do another,' said Ian trying to sound more upbeat than he felt.

Diane put her glass down and leant across the table. 'Are you mad? You want to put yourself through this again? The worry, the panic, the sleepless nights?'

'How do you—?'

'Come on, Ian. I've followed the sale, and I know you. I can see it in your face – you've been through hell.'

Ian put his head in his hands. 'But what choice do I have?'

'There are always choices, Ian,' Diane said sternly. 'And as it happens, I've made it easy for you. I bought the house.' She leant back in her chair, smiling smugly.

Ian felt the ground shifting under his feet as if reality had been suspended.

'You did what? But the estate agent said it was someone called Mr Beresford.'

'Yup, Tom Beresford, my business partner, remember? Once the sale has been completed, ownership will transfer to me.'

Anger and humiliation bubbled. 'You had no right to interfere!'

'I can buy whichever property I like. And anyway, I couldn't let Jerry ruin you, I've got an inheritance to protect for your neices.' She leant over and gave Ian a playful punch on the shoulder

Anger and humiliation was now laced with a smattering of relief, and Ian was speechless.

After a few rapid mouthfuls of wine, he looked suspiciously at Diane. 'Okay, so what are you going to do with it?'

'I'm guessing you don't want to live there as my tenant.' She smirked as Ian shuddered at the thought. 'I'll get it remodelled into something that will make the house an attractive investment for the lettings market, and then resell.'

Ian and Jerry's business partnership was dissolved within a few weeks, and their marriage followed suit a few months later. The ever laid-back Jerry wasted no time in mourning what they'd had, and cheerfully moved on, almost as if the whole thing had never happened.

Ian's previous employer took him back, apparently seeing his temporary absence as some kind of aberration, and Ian had never been so grateful for a guaranteed monthly salary.

A year or so later, Ian saw on Facebook that a house had collapsed in the same area as their ill-fated project. Fortunately, no one had been at home, and it later became apparent that faulty building work had been the cause. Jerry had breezed through the court case seemingly unaware that he had endangered lives, accepting the hefty fine with his usual indifference.

On the TV news, Ian had spotted himself reflected in the haunted face of Jerry's current 'partner' and thanked his lucky stars for Diane.

How long would it be before there was death on Jerry's hands, and would he still walk away with that nonchalant grin?

Originally published on https://cafelit.co.uk 13 September 2021

Goodbyes Mess With Your Head

WE MAKE OUR CAPPUCCINOS last. I don't suggest a second; I want this conversation to be over.

'You don't feel the same about me anymore, but there's no one else.'

I nod, desperate for him to accept what I've said. I know Owen well enough to be sure that there won't be a loud, embarrassing scene. That isn't his style.

'Come on, Mia. You know that's a load of crap. Remember, I know you inside out.' He drains his cup, replacing it carefully in the saucer. 'What aren't you telling me?'

I shift in my seat, looking down, trying to hide burning cheeks behind my hair. Why does Owen have to be...so...Owen?

What would Kath do? She would walk away without a backward glance. I straighten my spine, drawing my shoulders back. 'I can't see you anymore, Owen, and that's all there is to it. I'm sorry.'

Once I'm around the corner, my legs are shaking so badly that I sink to the ground.

'All sorted?' Kath sits beside me and offers me a drag on her cigarette. 'What did you tell him?'

'My fault not yours...all the usual crap.'

'Did he buy it?'

'No.'

'You should have just made a clean break. Good-byes always mess with your head.' She stands, pulling me to my feet. 'Come on, you've a flight to catch and I've got your new passport.'

Suddenly, I don't want to be like Kath – it's too scary.

'I'm not coming. I'm not doing this to Owen.'

'Doing this to Owen. For God's sake. After all he's done to you, Mia.'

I push her away and run back into the coffee shop.

'I knew you'd see sense.' He holds me tight and pinches my arm.

The Not-So-Secret Garden

LUCY HAD HATED HER grandfather for many years, even though she'd never met him. From unspecific family conversations, she'd grown to understand that he had been a controlling bully, although her grandmother would go no further than: 'My husband was a difficult man, you know,' safe in the dementia-fuelled belief that no one in her audience had known him. Lucy hated that her grandmother had endured such an unhappy and humiliating life, even though pride hadn't allowed her to admit it.

She knew that her mother had been frightened of Lucy's grandfather and had escaped by getting married and moving away as soon as she had finished university. Lucy knew this because her mother's cousin, Aunt Sal, had told her so one day, in a surprisingly frank conversation. But whenever Lucy had tried to talk to her mother about her childhood, the conversation would be firmly shut down. 'That's all in the past and there's no point in raking it all up now.'

But it wasn't all in the past, was it? The ripple effect of her grandfather's behaviour was still affecting the family now. As she got older, Lucy had come to realise that her mother's incapacity to show affection, either physically or otherwise, stemmed from her own dysfunctional upbringing; and that, in turn, had made Lucy into a needy, attention-seeking young woman. Following her suicide attempt, Lucy's first appointment with Ellen, her counsellor, had not gone well.

'Can you tell me a little bit about your journey to this point in your life?'

Silence.

'How are you feeling now?'

'I've just tried to cut my wrists, so pretty shitty, actually!'

Ellen looked at Lucy over the top of her glasses for a few moments.

'Have you seen anyone from your family since you've been in hospital?'

'My mum came and just acted as if I'd had my appendix out, or something. I don't even know where my dad is – he couldn't cope with living with an iceberg!' Lucy stood up. 'Look, are we done here? I've got a life to sort out.'

'Have you?'

Everything was falling to pieces in Lucy's head. Pieces she didn't know how to put back together. Ellen was right; what kind of life did she have? Lucy had dropped out of art college and was now working in her local branch of a national coffee chain – encouraging people to 'Go on, treat yourself.' She still sketched from time to time, but couldn't seem to face the hassle of getting all her paints and equipment out to do anything more. And anyway, she lived in a shared house where there was no room to leave things out. Her latest relationship had shrivelled and gone the way of many others, as her girlfriend had run for the hills when Lucy's possessive neediness had stifled any chance of happiness for either of them. She had one friend, Sophie; but Sophie had got her life together, finished uni, got a fellow architect as a partner, and was living it up with other bright young things in Brixton. Lucy had been left behind, and their lives were on different paths, although Lucy's life didn't seem to have a path to anywhere; she was stranded in an endless car park.

The sessions with Ellen eventually resumed, and somewhere deep down, Lucy knew she was lucky to have them – other people had to wait months for just six sessions. Paying for counselling was a sign that her mother had shown some recognition of Lucy's distress, albeit in a characteristically remote way – refusing to talk about it, and deflecting the conversation whenever Lucy mentioned Ellen. 'That's between you and her.'

As the appointments came round, Lucy found herself looking forward to the peaceful oasis that was Ellen's room. She could just sit and be still, not having to be anywhere or do anything, and sometimes she and Ellen would spend almost the whole hour in companionable silence. The best thing was that there was a huge, full-length window which looked out onto a garden where there was always something new to see as the weeks went by.

Eventually, Lucy found herself saying: 'I wish I could paint this, or even just draw it – look at the blossom on that apple tree. I keep thinking how I would paint it in watercolours, delicate and translucent against the blue sky.' She felt her cheeks redden. Had she really just said all that? Ellen would think she was pretentious and showing off, and Lucy cared about how Ellen saw her.

'So why don't you? Bring a sketch pad next time.'

That was the turning point. As the weeks went by, sketching turned into painting and Lucy and Ellen talked about anything and everything, although on reflection, Lucy realised that it was mostly herself talking about anything and everything. She found that while she was painting, she stopped worrying about what to say, about what Ellen thought of her, and the floodgates opened.

Ellen never commented on her work, never even referred to it. Her go-to phrase seemed to be, 'Tell me more about...' nudging Lucy on. Maybe she had left the car park, but Lucy had no idea where she was headed.

By the time she was painting the first frost of the year, Lucy knew that she had reached a point where she was ready to think about what might be next in her life. 'I really want to do something with my life. I want to help people deal with the crap in their past so that they don't end up like me.'

'Maybe you mean, so that they don't go through what you've been through,' said Ellen gently.

'Well, whatever...'

'Maybe you could use your art to tell people something.'

'It's only dabbling, I don't think anyone would gain anything from looking at those.' Lucy gestured towards the bulging sketchbook.

In a rare, quiet, afternoon at the shared house, Lucy got her pictures out and looked at them. Maybe they could tell a story; the story of her journey through a garden. Her housemate, Ben, worked at one of those artists' hubs sponsored by a mental-health charity; maybe she could have a word with him. Something visceral inside Lucy told her this was the way to go, even though she didn't think she had a cat-in-hell's chance of actually mounting an exhibition.

But Ben had been surprisingly enthusiastic.

'Wow, Lucy, what an amazing idea. I didn't know you were an artist! Can I see some of your pictures?'

'Sure, they're only watercolours done on a sketch pad though.'

Ben looked through some examples that Lucy showed him, and called Janey, another house resident, to come and have a look. 'Wow, you're a dark horse, Lucy! My God, these are amazing!'

Ben arranged a meeting with the hub manager, a stern-looking woman called Lorraine. 'Ben tells me you've got an idea for an exhibition. He seems very enthusiastic. Can you tell me more?'

'Well, I just thought maybe I could show the pictures as a kind of mental-health journey or something. I did them during my counselling sessions – my counsellor has an amazing garden,' she added.

'Okay, well let's have a look at them and see what we can do.'

As Lorriane looked through, Lucy babbled nervously: 'I don't have any money to frame them or anything, and I'm not looking to make any money… I just want to help people really.'

Eventually, Lorraine looked up and took a deep breath.

'Oh my God, here goes... the big N. O.,' said Lucy to herself, already stuffing her paintings back into their case.

'Lucy, I love your idea, and these paintings... Well...they're unique. I think we should turn the whole hub into an exhibition of your work for two weeks over Easter. We'll pay for any framing and other expenses. Your job is to select fifteen or twenty paintings, or sketches, that best illustrate your journey. Maybe you could write something to go with them. What do you think?'

Lucy stared at Lorraine. 'Are you serious?'

'Too right I'm serious, sweetie. So you'd better get cracking!'

Lucy debated with herself whether to tell her mother and the rest of the family about the exhibition. Her mother would probably tell her that she was showing off. But suddenly, Lucy came to the knowledge that she didn't care what her mother thought – that who she was, wasn't defined by what other people thought of her – even Ellen, so she invited everyone she could think of. Lucy liked that the exhibition was for a cause that was bigger than her.

Six weeks later, on the opening night, Lucy stood, hands clenched behind her back, waiting to see if anyone would turn up. The doors opened and a crowd flooded in. Lucy spotted all her house mates, Lorraine and all the new friends she'd made at the hub, even Ellen, and...her mother. While surrounded by well-wishers offering their congratulations, Lucy covertly kept an eye on her mother, who had been taking time to gaze at every picture on show. She had expected her to take a quick glance, say a cursory 'Well done,' and fade away into the night. But no, she was actually *looking*...no, studying, Lucy's work.

Ellen came over and patted Lucy's back. 'You did it, Lucy!'

Lucy hugged her. 'Thank you so much for being on this journey with me and allowing me to experience your garden.'

'Well, you know where I am if you need to visit again, any time.' Ellen hugged Lucy back.

Eventually Lucy plucked up the courage to stand beside her mother, and was shocked to see tears running down her cheeks. 'Oh, Mum...' She put an arm around her and held her close.

Helen turned and put a hand up to Lucy's face, cupping her cheek. 'I never knew how to talk to you, but it seems, you know how to talk to me. Lucy, these are beautiful, and I'm so sorry about the life I gave you.'

'But you *gave* me a life, that's the main thing,' said Lucy, risking a joke.

Helen smiled and squeezed her hand.

'And I'm sorry about the life you had, growing up,' Lucy added.

'I guess we're all part of a chain – I'm sure your grandfather had someone in his life who made him equally unhappy and who stunted his growth, but we'll never know who, and it doesn't matter now. The important thing is that we recognise what has happened and learn from it. It's taken until now, and learning about your journey, for me to realise that.'

Helen paused. 'And your grandfather wasn't always a bad-tempered ogre; he loved his garden, and on good days I can remember seeing him drawing and sketching – even painting in his later years.'

More of the fragments of who she was came together in Lucy's mind. 'So, I get this from him?' she said, gesturing at the pictures.

'Yes, you do. And to be honest, I've been so busy trying to forget about him, that I'd forgotten about those fleeting good times, when he was happy, painting and drawing in the garden. Of course, he would never talk about it, and we never found any of his work. I think he just destroyed everything; it was maybe his private thing that he didn't want to share.'

Lucy couldn't quite get her head around this new mother, and honestly wondered if she was dreaming. But if she was, she certainly didn't want to wake up. In this world, she had a real life and her own path. She also had Carrie, another artist at the hub, who was sending her positive vibes from behind the drinks table. Lucy could feel them without looking at her.

When Lucy's grandmother died – in blissful ignorance of the Covid pandemic raging outside, and inside, the nursing home – Lucy helped her mother sort through the remains of her small life. Over this heart-breaking task, Helen and Lucy got to know each other, and Lucy was astonished to learn that her mother had been seeing a man called Brian for years, and that they had been on several cruises together. 'Wow, I'm really going to have to keep an eye on you, Mum, gallivanting off with all and sundry.'

'Brian is not "all and sundry," I'll have you know,' Helen said archly.

Lucy laughed out of sheer pleasure that her mother was having a good life, and before she knew it, the unthinkable happened and they were giggling together like a couple of teenagers.

'Honestly, Mum,' gasped Lucy, drying her tears.

As they were packing the last few books, Lucy noticed a folded piece of A4 nestling between two pages. She opened it out and gasped in surprise. Here was her apple tree, painted just as she'd imagined it, the blossom delicate against a brilliant blue sky.

The book that followed on from the exhibition included Lucy's grandfather's painting next to her own version. She had the originals mounted, side by side, in a single frame, and wondered whether her grandfather was happy at last.

Originally published on https://cafelit.co.uk/ 3 September 2021

Away from Prying Eyes

'NEVER OPEN THAT DOOR,' my landlord said to me the day I moved into 22 New Street. He never gave an explanation, and I was too excited about moving into my first house to ask. Absorbed in unpacking and setting up my new home, I didn't give it a thought until a few weeks later.

The ticking started one evening just after *East Enders*. I muted the TV and listened. The noise was definitely coming from the hallway. Heart pounding, I approached the forbidden door. The ticking was rhythmic – like a clock...or a bomb.

As I put my ear to the stripped pine the sound stopped. Shaking my head, I returned to *Holby City*, where the love-life of one of the consultants soon put any thoughts of what was behind the door to the back of my mind. After all, it wasn't anything to do with me, was it?

The following Saturday afternoon, I heard it again, louder this time. I abandoned my cake mix in the kitchen and approached the door with day-time confidence. Disobeying, I turned the handle and was surprised when the catch released. I jumped back in shock, hurriedly pushing the door closed as an incoming text alert recalled me to the kitchen.

I said to never open that door!

I froze, still holding the phone, the implications swirling in my head. When I dared to move my head, I scanned the kitchen – there were no cameras that I could see. I summoned up the courage to approach the door again, phone in hand. Looking around the hall, I could see no evidence of any sur-veillance. Another text arrived:

You won't find anything, but it's not just you who has prying eyes.

Originally published in *Secret Attic Anthology #21* December 2021

Am-Dram Antics

IT WAS HALFWAY THROUGH the second act when Rob forgot his lines. He could hear Sonia's stage-whispered prompt from the wings, but the words meant nothing. Leading lady, Amelia, glared at him, willing him to say something, but Rob was suspended in a timeless freeze-frame...until the spell was broken by a ripple of coughing and fidgeting from the audience.

'Nothing to say, Gerald?' Acid Amelia had never been good at improvisation.

'I'm not Gerald, for God's sake! Let's all stop acting and have some truth for once.' Rob turned to Amelia. 'When are you going to tell John about you and Sonia?'

Teddy Bear Chaos

EMMA STUDIED THE INSTALLATION with a critical eye. She couldn't help thinking the bears arranged on a set of steps looked a little drunk. She found the twenty-five toothless grins unsettling. Shouldn't bears have those cute little sewn-on mouths? The bear in the middle of the stairs, however, seemed completely unfazed by the craziness around it, having an almost life-like appearance. It was as if the rest of the bears on the side-lines didn't count.

'Okaa-y, I've seen it all now!' Coral's husky voice drew Emma back to the moment. 'What is all that about?'

'It's going to be a nightmare to manage,' added Emma. 'Have you read the guide?'

'It's nuts – apparently it's an "interactive" thing (Coral made air quotes). So, anyone can rearrange the bears, but they have to take a picture to post on the gallery Facebook page and write on one of these forms about why and how they've arranged them?'

'Yup. That's about it. The artist has completed one for his arrangement, and his comments are over there on the wall with a picture.'

Coral strode across and read aloud:

> *The arrangement shows my view of society. Most people are content to be on the side-lines because they're either too apathetic, bored or preoccupied with the small stuff in life. But there are those that need to be centre stage, to have the limelight. These are the most alive.*

'No prizes for guessing who he identifies with then. What a dick. Without the boring, "side-liners" like us, beavering away in the background, there would be no installation would there!'

Emma was surprised at Coral's angry tone. She was usually so laid-back. 'Well, it'll be entertaining, that's for sure! You off now?'

'Yep, I'm out with the girls tonight.'

'See you bright and early tomorrow then.'

Emma finished locking up, set the alarm, and headed for the bus stop, looking forward to a takeaway and a cosy night in with Netflix.

Emma and Coral were uniformed and ready for action by 9 a.m. the next morning. They had several rooms to manage, so were taking it in turns with the bears.

Emma had volunteered for the first two hours. They were often quiet as most people didn't arrive until around eleven-ish. A few early visitors came and stared at the installation, read the artists notes, and moved swiftly on. Coral noted much the same, over lunch. People seemed strangely reluctant to move the bears, or even touch them.

The idea of interfering with a work of art was obviously a step too far for most.

The next day was different. It was the weekend, when it seemed that those with fewer inhibitions visited. A couple holding hands, maybe on a first date, Emma thought, moved another one of the other bears to the centre, pushing others carelessly out of the way. When they had taken the obligatory selfie and had moved on, she read:

> *We two are the centre of our world because those who are in love are the special ones.*

'God! Who do they think they are? Anthony and Cleopatra?' said Coral when Emma showed her the new arrangement at lunchtime. 'Let's see what they write after six months.'

Then came an older woman, who having stood motionless in front of the installation for some time, suddenly strode forward and pushed all the bears into the middle and placed one in a dark corner at the top of the stairs almost hidden from sight. As she didn't have a mobile, she asked Emma to take the obligatory picture and post it on 'wherever it needs to go' for her. Tears in her eyes, she had written:

> *This is me – I'm invisible while everyone else gets on with their busy lives. I used to be important too.*

Emma wondered what her story was, and whether it would ever be told.

From then on, the bears went through much choreography and by the end of the day were looking rather the worse for wear. Under strict instructions not to touch them or interfere with the installation, Emily and Coral left them to their own devices and went home.

Emma was surprised to see Coral already in the staffroom with a cup of coffee the next morning. Usually, she scooted in with just enough time to change into her uniform and be at her post for 9 a.m.

'Wow, what happened to you? Is that Irn Bru in your coffee?'

'There was something I needed to do before the others got here.' There was a grim satisfaction in the way Coral sipped her coffee, leaning back in the chair. 'Take a look for yourself – Room 3.'

Emma felt a strange prickle of foreboding as she approached the bears.

They were still crazily arranged over the stairs, left by the family with hordes of children who had been the last after-school visitors, yesterday. But this morning their heads were grinning at her from a pile on the floor.

'My God, Coral! What have you done?' Emma turned, sensing Coral's presence behind her.

'I've re-arranged the installation, just like the artist wanted. It's amazing what you can do with a pair of gardening shears.'

'I don't think—'

'I just wanted to show that pretentious bastard what I really felt about all this crap. Sometimes those of us on the side-lines need to have our say.'

Emma stared at Coral.

Coral's Facebook post went viral after that final morning at the gallery, and there were a number of supportive comments:

Good on you! Thank you for showing what we all think, secretly.

Hats off to you (laughing emoji)

That's told all those posh, pretentious arty types. What do they know about real life, anyway!

When the artist was contacted for comment, his response was: 'The installation did exactly what it was supposed to do. Be provocative and generate discussion. It took a while and I had to get a couple of friends in to get the ball rolling. I just didn't expect the violence to escalate so quickly.'

Chance Escape

SHOULD I SUFFER IN silence, or should I flee? I won't miss his aftershave smell, or the night-time visitors. I throw a dice and it lands on Go! The decision is made for me. Packing is a brief activity – a few essentials in a backpack, and I'm ready.

I get as far as the pavement when that bitch Linda sees me. She pins me against the wall, fishing for her phone and I know it's all over.

But then, from nowhere, a taxi arrives. 'Go,' she says, thrusting a bunch of notes into my pocket.

Perhaps she isn't such a bitch after all.

Originally published as *Chance of Freedom* in Secret Attic Booklet #26 February 2022

Take a Seat

'COME IN AND TAKE a seat, Sally.'

Sally obediently does as she's told and sits perched on the edge of the chair, ready for flight.

'How are you doing today?'

'I'm okay.' She keeps her gaze fixed on the man mowing the lawn outside the window. The sound is soothing, a dishonest sign of normality.

'Jackie says you've not been eating much.'

Sally knows where this is going, a familiar road where the nurse reports back to the doctor, and if she doesn't get her act together, they will feed her anyway. Her body is not her own.

She wonders what sort of life the man stolidly walking up and down with the mower has. What does he worry about? Whatever it is, she would give anything to be him in this moment.

'Sally... Are you listening?' She is wrenched back to the sterile consulting room.

'Sorry. Yes.'

'So, we need to get you eating. Yes? Remember the strategies we've worked on?'

'Yes.'

'Okay, well I'll see you again on Friday.'

Sally knows she'll do what they want – in the end.

Friday comes; it's raining and no one is mowing the lawn.

'How are you doing, Sally?'

'Okay, I guess.'

'I'm pleased to hear from Jackie that you've been much better. Keep it up.'

Sally doesn't feel much better and refuses to make eye contact – one small rebellion.

It's Friday again, and there is a different doctor. Sally hasn't seen this one before.

'Would you like to sit down, Sally?'

She has a choice? This is new. Sally chooses to stand.

'Can you tell me what we can do to help you feel better?'

Sally considers. 'Could I go out sometimes?'

'Of course.'

'On my own?'

'Why not?'

Sally savours the moment before turning to look at the doctor. 'I just need to be free.'

When the Fun Stops...

JUST ONE MORE. CASSIE still had twenty minutes until she had to pick the kids up from school.

She pressed Play and waited, holding her breath.

Sorry, you haven't won this time. She'd got this far – she had to win eventually, surely!

When the Fun Stops, Stop! The words blinked at her from the top of the screen, and Cassie huffed in irritation, knowing that this is precisely the point at which you *can't* stop. Okay, just time for a few more turns. She topped up her account feeling a sense that this was going to be when her luck changed. She felt great!

Somewhere on the edge of her consciousness, Cassie noticed that the school was trying to get through on her phone. Oh shit! Where had all that time gone?

'Hello, is that Amelia and Seb's mum?'

'Yes, I'm so sorry. I should be there in about five minutes. The traffic is dreadful.' The words spilled out and Cassie rang off before the imperious school secretary could say anything else. It wasn't the first time.

Racing through the school gate, she was confronted with one mutinous eleven-year-old and a tearful five-year-old. 'It's like you don't care about us! You don't even have to go to work,' snapped Amelia.

'I'm so sorry. I'll make it up to you.'

'That's what you always say. I hate you.'

'And that's when I knew I had to get help.' Cassie looked up at the group, already feeling their support.

Blast from the Past

'THAT'S WHERE I KNOW him from.'

Becca stood up, the chair crashing to the ground behind her.

'Becca, wait!' said Lorna.

But Becca didn't wait. She strode over to the men grouped around a table on the other side of the pub.

They carried on laughing and joking, not noticing her angry approach.

'You!' Becca jabbed at him with her finger. The tall, powerfully built man turned in annoyance.

'What the...?'

'I know you, you bastard!'

By now some of his group were on their feet. 'Now come on, lady. What's your problem?'

'Who the hell are you?' the target of Becca's outrage replied not bothering to get up.

You don't even remember me, *Ryan*, do you? Well I'm not the push-over I was back then, so maybe you need reminding of what you did to me.

Ryan gestured to his friends that this was some mad woman, not to be taken seriously.

'Okay, so your memory is so short that you don't remember raping me when we were at school. Or maybe you've done it so many times that I didn't even register.'

There were gasps of shock and a few dismissive laughs as the encounter grabbed everyone's attention.

'What the hell are you going on about? Wishful thinking, I reckon!' he smirked.

Becca stood tall and addressed the group. 'This man raped me when I was fourteen, on school premises, during a lunch break. I was so ashamed, I didn't tell anyone. I'm pretty sure I wasn't his only victim.' Ryan's friends looked at him uncertainly, although one or two still seemed to think it was great entertainment.

'No, you weren't.' A voice behind Becca spoke clearly and decisively. 'He did it to me too.' Becca turned and locked eyes with her sister.

Originally published in *Secret Attic Booklet #14* May 2020

Maxine and Jenny

MAXINE HUMMED PART OF a Chopin Nocturne, idly noticing the washing dancing a tarantella on the line in the courtyard as she waited for the soup to heat up in the microwave. Three minutes. Jenny would have tutted at such a waste of time. 'Think of all the things you could have done in those three minutes.' Maxine could still hear the disapproving voice.

After the *ping*, she took the soup with a plate of bread and butter and sat at the kitchen table. Maxine couldn't remember the last time she'd turned the oven on – all her food was microwaved these days. Tonight's supper would be tinned chilli with the rice that came in those handy sachets. Another three-minute meal.

Wanting to escape Jenny, Maxine returned to the adventures of Becky Sharp on her e-reader as she munched and swallowed her way through lunch. Half an hour later, she was still engrossed in *Vanity Fair*, where Becky was now the belle of London society while busily ignoring her son. Maxine had learnt at an early age that a good book was a sure-fire way of switching Jenny off, and as she got older, she found that playing the piano had the same effect. Sighing, she put Becky to one side and considered the next three or four hours. She could go for a walk, play some more Chopin, bring the washing in and put it away – Maxine never did ironing – or carry on reading. Or she could...

Shaking her head and banging her hands flat on the table, Maxine levered herself up from the chair, and, leaving the lunch things where they were in an unseen act of defiance, slowly mounted the stairs to Jenny's room. She had put on weight since working from home, something else Jenny had never failed to mention. 'Why don't you get out and go for a walk, or join a gym or something, Maxine, instead of letting yourself go?' But rewarding herself with little snacks now and again helped structure the day and break up the time.

Even though Jenny had not visited the room for two months and would not be coming back, Maxine knew that it would always be filled with her unseen presence. Even walking past the closed door to her own bedroom still took an effort of will, even after all these weeks. It was almost as if some essence of Jenny could seep under the door onto the landing. But today, somehow, it was time to grasp the nettle, face facts, feel the fear, or whatever the next cliché might be. It was now or never.

Maxine stopped to get her breath and steadied herself on the bannister rail. She counted to ten, and then, taking a deep breath and holding it, she turned the knob and felt the door stick before it yielded to the weight of her body. As it gave, Maxine paused for the briefest of moments before opening the door wide and taking a step into the room.

There was a hint of Jenny's perfume still hanging in the air as Maxine strode purposefully to the window and slid up the sash to take some strength from the reassuring sound of the birds and the traffic from outside. She could hear her next-door neighbour, Jack, and Bill from across the road having their usual, shouty, conversation. Neither was deaf, but it seemed they only had one volume setting. Today they were yelling to each other about the Covid restrictions and whether Bill and Linda would be able to get away in their caravan any time soon. Maxine stood out of sight, away from the window, taking strength from the mundane lives of Jack and Bill.

The first thing she noticed when she turned to face the room was the neatly made bed – just as Jenny would have liked it. Maxine opened the wardrobe door and took a hasty step back as everything that was Jenny threatened to overwhelm her and somehow pull her in.

She took a deep breath and willed herself to look at Jenny's clothes hanging neatly in seasonal order, her polished shoes in the rack under the shelf where her small collection of handbags rested. Jenny, disapproving of extravagance, had bought only items she deemed essential – the basics for each season, plus her spare police sergeant's uniform. The only exception being an uncharacteristically flamboyant dress purchased for a holiday they had never taken.

Maxine realised that her hand was shaking as she reached out to touch the jeans that Jenny had been wearing the last time she'd seen her alive. This small movement was a victory and Maxine felt emboldened to explore the wardrobe further, pushing the hanging clothes along the rack to reveal two wooden boxes stacked along the back panel. She froze for a moment, expecting Jenny's angry admonishment: 'What do you think you're doing, Maxine? Who said you could look through my private things? Who do you think you are?' But that hadn't stopped Jenny looking through Maxine's drawers and finding hidden letters from their father, had it? It hadn't stopped her from tearing them into tiny pieces as Maxine had looked helplessly on.

She managed to wrestle the two unwieldy boxes from the back of the wardrobe and onto the bed. No longer caring about the wrinkled quilt cover, Maxine sat and tried to open the lid of first one and then the other, but they were both locked. She didn't remember ever having seen them before; they looked antique, with marquetry designs on the sides and lids, and beautifully crafted metal locks. Maxine, no longer caring about tidiness, rummaged through the bedside drawers searching for the two small keys that would open the boxes. Eventually, in the bottom drawer behind a neatly arranged row of socks she discovered a small leather pouch, and there were the keys.

Without hesitating she tried one of the keys in the first box and it opened easily – evidence of regular use. Maxine lifted the lid cautiously as if some part of Jenny might somehow jump out like the Jack-in-a-Box she'd hated as a child. Inside she found a pile of brown envelopes, a cheap pad of writing paper, a Pritt stick, a pair of scissors and a number of folded magazine and newspaper pages. She laid them out on the bed and considered. Then, using the second key, she opened the second, heavier, box. This time, there was a camera, a sim card, and a notebook filled with dates, times and addresses.

Maxine felt an ominous tickling creep over her scalp as she picked up the camera, switched it on and flicked through some of the photos. There was Mandy from down the road in a clinch with Jack, obviously captured from outside her lounge window, in spite of the partly closed blinds. Then she saw a short film clip of Jenny's colleague, Beth, surreptitiously putting a lipstick in her bag and walking out of the shop. Maxine flicked on to pictures and clips of people she didn't recognise, all of whom, seemingly, had secrets to hide.

As if contaminated by some kind of toxin, Maxine threw the camera on the bed and recoiled in horror.

Clasping her hands behind her neck, she took some deep breaths and looked at the darkening clouds outside the window. Jack and Bill had long since finished shouting at one another, apparently having retreated indoors. She heard a distant siren and wondered who else's day was not going as planned.

Leaving everything on the bed, Maxine went back onto the landing, quietly closing the door behind her.

Bach Preludes and Fugues were usually good for times of stress, as Maxine could lose herself in the intricate repeating patterns between the different lines, but having played three straight off in a row, she didn't feel the usual soothing effect. So, instead, after a cup of tea and several pieces of cake, she turned to Netflix and watched a few episodes of a new box set she'd saved.

That evening the clouds thickened and the heavens opened. The neglected washing drooped disconsolately on the line as Maxine microwaved her chilli and rice. She sat at the table to eat, pushing the dishes from lunch to one side with the sweep of her arm. Surprisingly, she found herself to be very hungry and tucked in to the comforting warmth of the food.

Having stacked the dishes in the dishwasher, Maxine returned to the living room, planning to return to the comforting misfortunes of someone other than herself, in *Vanity Fair*. But this time even reading couldn't help her escape from Jenny. In spite of all Maxine's usual avoidance tactics, she loomed larger than ever. Tossing Becky and Amelia aside, with an okay-you-win sigh, Maxine stared at the curtains, closed against the water falling outside, and cast her mind back over the last few months. Had there been any clue about Jenny's toxic covert activities that she had missed? Jenny had always worked random hours so she could have come and gone without Maxine thinking anything of it. Her police surveillance training had obviously come in handy for her covert hobby!

An unusual sense of superiority was creeping over Maxine. How had Jenny dared criticise and complain about Maxine, when her own little life had been so sad and pathetic? In fact, when Maxine thought about it, Jenny had complained about and criticised everyone. Maybe the roots of this poison lay as far back as when their father had left their domineering and controlling mother. Jenny had never forgiven him – everything was black and white for her. People were either good or bad (mostly bad) and there was no grey area in between. Over the last year, Maxine had made contact with their father. They had written real letters to each other which Maxine had been strangely thrilled by, and had then taken to meeting on a regular basis. He told her what life had been like with their violent mother and how, almost fearing for his life, he had had to leave. He had worried about Jenny and Maxine for years but had never been allowed anywhere near them.

When Covid allowed, a few weeks later, Maxine drove to meet her father.

'Well, would you believe it?' Alan said when he heard about Jenny's sordid little secret.

They drank their coffees in silence for a few minutes, both revelling in the simple pleasure of meeting for coffee and cake after the long, dark, isolated, months of a Covid winter.

'What are you going to do about it? asked Alan, eventually, replacing his empty cup in its saucer.

'Do about it? What do you mean...do about it?'

'Well, will you tell the police? Let them notify all these people, whoever they are?'

'Why should I? They were all doing something they shouldn't have been. And Jenny's not coming back, so it's not like she can be arrested or anything.'

'I suppose...'

'And anyway, I don't want to be involved with anything she did.' Maxine made a pushing away gesture with her arm. 'I want her out of my life.'

'And how is that working out for you, now that you've got rid of her?' Alan fixed her with a steely stare.

Maxine shifted slightly in her chair. 'What are you on about? She's the one that wrapped her car around a tree.'

'Do you know she actually came to see me a few weeks before the accident?' Alan's gaze was still fixed on Maxine.

"*What?* You never said!'

'She didn't want you to know. She was scared.'

'Scared of what?'

'You.'

Originally published in *Glittery Literary Anthology 3* September 2021

The Beach of Disgrace

ROBERT LAID HIS HEAD back on the cushion. He could hear children in the distance; it must be playtime. He tried to take himself back to a time when he would have given anything to be sitting at home on a Wednesday morning with a strong coffee and the crossword, the stresses of school far away.

He imagined Gina scanning the playground, clutching her non-spill, re-useable cup, anxiously expecting the worst, while tall, athletic Gil strode an effortless path through the sea of children, casual as you like. Robert heard the faint sound of the bell he had rung hundreds of times, and then silence descended broken only by the distant hum of a glinting, silver bird, high up in the sky, the passengers enjoying their high-altitude coffee and snacks.

He studied the sky, tracking wispy clouds through the glass roof of the conservatory. Was he the only person in the world not doing something? The only person serving no useful purpose? Robert knew this wasn't true, but sometimes the feeling of being left behind was overwhelming. Just as the ripple of death rocks those closest to the epicentre and lessens its effect as it spreads until there is hardly any evidence of a departing, and the world simply carries on. But Robert wasn't dead, he was living, suspended in a kind of chrysalis while the world went on without him. His 'inner child' as Nicola called it wanted to shout, 'Stop! Wait for me!' But he was trapped and couldn't move.

Suspension had come swiftly and unexpectedly. The chair of governors making an unplanned visit.

'This is a surprise, Donald. What can I do for you?'

Donald had shifted his tall frame in the too-small chair, his knees edging up towards his chin. Robert always liked his visitors to be on lower chairs than his own and suppressed a smile. Donald cleared his throat, the prominent Adam's apple bobbing nervously. 'Well, Robert... The thing is we've had a complaint.'

'Right.' Nothing unusual about that.

'It's just that...well the Blacks have written to Ofsted.'

In an instant, all sorts of alarm bells started ringing at the very mention of the dreaded 'O' word.

Robert leant forward. 'Tell me.'

'Apparently Kayden told them that you hit him with a ruler when you kept him in at playtime yesterday.' Donald fidgeted with a button on his jacket. 'There was a mark on his arm.'

It was true, he *had* hit Kayden with a ruler. What had he been thinking? He'd been annoyed at having to spend the twenty minutes of break time with the boy. Normally, it wouldn't have bothered him, but yesterday, Robert had been behind in preparing for a meeting with the academy management and stress had got the better of him. It hadn't been a hard swipe, just a tap, really. He hadn't thought Kayden was the sort of child to whinge to his parents, who thought nothing of giving him the odd slap themselves. The more Robert thought about it, the more the whole thing made his blood boil – that such a small thing should ruin what had been a solid, successful career since he had been made head teacher three years earlier.

In that moment, as Donald spoke, Robert's world had collapsed, the following Ofsted inspection a blur in which he had played no part. And now, here he was, waiting for the results of an enquiry, washed up with the flotsam and jetsam of scandal regardless of the outcome. Nicola had left, although Robert suspected that this was the excuse she had long been looking for. The house was up for sale and an uncertain future awaited him.

What happened to those marooned on the Beach of Disgrace? Robert imagined that many took to any substance or activity that would blot out the reality. They didn't care what people thought anymore; they had nothing to lose. Others took the short cut to oblivion by taking their own lives. But…maybe there were a few who eventually got the energy from somewhere to crawl up the beach and somehow find a way back.

Robert still had a lot of living to do, hadn't he? And he was blowed if he was going to let the likes of Kayden Black ruin his life. There had to be a way forward, a different path; there had to be a way. He stood up and strode into the no-longer shared study, sat at his desk and pulled the lap-top towards him.

A glance out of the window at the suburban, day-time quiet of Water Lane and Robert was away. Down the lane, along the ring-road, past the industrial estate and onto the motorway…to where?

Flexing his hands and stretching his arms, Robert readied himself for action. A burst of rapid typing revealed a wide selection of campervans.

After a few YouTube tutorials and advice from Derek-next-door, a seasoned campervanner and cyclist, Robert was ready. Having realised there was very little in the house of any real significance, he was travelling light, an excitement he hadn't felt since childhood bubbling in his stomach. He hadn't ridden a bike for thirty years and admired it, secure in its bike rack on the back of the van. Having given in his notice, there was nothing to hold him back. Was it really possible to start life all over again at forty-five?

There was no plan beyond heading for the motorway.

North or south? South – somewhere unfamiliar.

Robert found chugging aimlessly along the inside lane in the campervan strangely soporific and whole sections of the journey seemed to pass without registering in his memory. When it got to around 5.30, however, he thought it was time to find a camp site. Having tried several he found that campervanning was everybody's new, favourite pastime, as they were all full. Just as the first niggle of worry was starting to worm its way into his thoughts, he found the Windmill Campsite. It had vacancies but no windmill.

Having wisely brought a few provisions to tide himself over the first few days, Robert made beans on toast, and, as the sun was shining, he set his table and chair up outside, under the awning. It was the best beans on toast ever, swilled down with a fairly expensive Chardonnay. Robert sat back and sighed in contentment, closing his eyes and enjoying the unconditional warmth of the sun. The sun didn't always just shine on the righteous, he thought.

'A bit extravagant. A whole bottle of that just for one?'

Robert jumped, his glasses falling onto the table. Once they were back in place, a tall, elderly woman came into focus.

'Sorry?'

'I just said that it seems a bit extravagant – a whole bottle of that for one person.' She gestured at the half-empty bottle.

Robert had planned on having the other half the following night, but now it seemed rude not to share it. 'Take a seat and help me finish it,' he said gallantly, and having retrieved a second chair from the campervan and seated himself opposite his tall, elegant visitor.

'Thank you...'

'Robert. You're welcome...'

'Evelyn.' Evelyn smiled and leant forward to shake his hand.

Formalities over, they sat in silence enjoying the wine. It tasted better when shared, Robert decided.

'Are you here for long?'

'I don't know. To be honest, I'm making this journey up as I go along.'

'Good for you. I hate planned trips. That's the great thing about this.' Evelyn gestured around the site.

'Which is yours?' Robert was uncertain about campsite etiquette.

'Oh I don't have one.'

'Oh...?' the unspoken question hovered between them.

Evelyn laughed and replaced her glass on the table. 'That always gets everybody. I'm the owner and I live over there.' She tilted her head towards the entrance building. 'Above the office.'

'Right.'

'But don't get me wrong, I've done my time in tents, caravans and campervans, but there comes a time when it's best to hang up one's tow bar gracefully.

'Shall we finish this up?' Robert poured the rest of the wine.

'You're just the kind of person I set this site up for. I never take advance bookings, so all the wanderers end up here.'

Evelyn leant back, cradling the glass in her hands. 'So what are you running away from?'

'Sorry?' Robert, affronted at this personal question from someone he had only just met, put on his headteacher's voice. 'I don't think that's—'

'Oh but it is, Robert, because you are on my campsite, so I get to ask the questions.

By the time darkness had fallen, Robert had told his story, leaving nothing out, not even the growing indignation he felt about how he had been treated by Kayden, the Blacks, Donald and the board of governors, Ofsted, Nicola...the list was extensive.

'That's a lot of people who seem to have it in for you, Robert,' observed Evelyn, a silhouette in the darkness.

'Absolutely,' he returned, pleased that someone at last understood how badly he'd been treated.

'But... I can't help thinking that maybe those people have a reason to be unhappy with you, too. I don't pretend to know how schools – or marriages – work. I've avoided both. But I do know a lot about people.'

Robert's smug pleasure evaporated in a moment. 'I don't know what you mean,' he said standing abruptly, almost tipping the flimsy table over.

'I've been where you are. I know that feeling of uselessness and being left behind.' Evelyn was standing now, an urgency in her voice. 'And I can tell you that until you revisit that disgrace with an open heart, you won't find the path off the beach.'

Robert froze the half-folded table in his hand. 'How do you...?'

'Know about the Beach of Disgrace? Everyone who has been there recognises it, Robert. Thanks for the wine.'

Open-mouthed, he watched her outline vanish into the darkness.

A long, restless night of reckoning followed. Not what Robert had expected for his first night in the campervan – the peaceful sleep of the free. Because he wasn't free, was he? Evelyn was right.

The following morning saw him at the outside table typing several emails. He apologised to the Blacks, Donald and the Board of Governors for letting them down and betraying their trust in him. There was no excuse for his behaviour – he understood that now.

Writing to Nicola took more thought. Where he had gone wrong in their marriage wasn't as clear cut. In the end, he wished her luck in her new life and told her to keep whatever she needed from the wreckage of their shared life together.

He took the laptop over to the office intending to connect to the wi-fi, expecting to see Evelyn somewhere around. He wanted to thank her for making him see things differently.

Eventually after much ringing of the bell on the counter a surly girl appeared, phone in hand. 'Yeah?'

'Can I have the wi-fi code? I need to send some emails.'

The girl nodded her head towards a notice on the wall, where, along with various campsite information was the password, printed in very small type at the bottom of the list. Internet usage was obviously not encouraged among the campers.

'I wonder if I could speak to Evelyn.'

'Evelyn who?' The girl shifted the gum to the other side of her mouth, her eyes still fixed on her phone.

'Evelyn, the owner of the site.' Robert was aware of the impatience in his voice – the same impatience that had been there in school when a child or member of staff had not agreed with him or hadn't understood what was required. He felt ashamed and was just starting to imagine how he had made those in his power feel.

'There's no Evelyn here. My dad owns the site.' She jerked her head towards the door where a large, thickset man was approaching.

'Excuse me. I need to speak to Evelyn – I know she's the owner of the site in spite of what this girl says.'

'You be careful how you talk about my daughter.' Robert suddenly felt at a disadvantage, not being on his own territory – not being the one who called the shots.

'Tell her, Dad. There – is – no – Evelyn.' She enunciated each word with venom.

'No Evelyn,' the big man concurred. 'Are you ready to settle up? Maybe it's time you moved on.'

Robert's campervanning took him to Cornwall, Wales, Scotland, even the outer Hebrides. He found that the UK was a place of surprising beauty and variety. On cycle rides he revelled in the summits of hills and even mountains, descended into valleys and followed the paths of rivers, he strode across moorland, and visited many cliffs and beaches along the way. His journey was a thoughtful one, and as he travelled the tumour of self-pity shrank, along with its inevitable companion, anger. In its place appeared small shoots of empathy and kindness. And Robert found that he could cope with not being in charge.

At the end of the year, although there was much journeying still to come, Robert could see a path leading off the Beach of Disgrace. A path that would allow him to lift his head up again, and to grow. He would always be grateful to his saviour, Evelyn, whoever she was.

Escape to the Tea Shop

STAN AND I DECIDED to make a break for it, to escape from Sunset Towers. We'd planned well ahead, the day before, and both stuffed our pockets with fruit and rolls at breakfast. Stan knew the code to open the door, and before we knew it we were out on the pavement.

'Okay, Batman, where shall we go first?'

'Oh, the seafront I think. Aren't all retirement homes near the sea?'

'Well, let's find out.'

We made slow progress, Stan with his Zimmer frame and me with my walking stick.

After what seemed like an age of walking, there was still no sign of the sea.

'I know, let's stop someone and ask.'

'Good thinking, Batman.'

We stopped the next person that came along, a youth in scruffy jeans. 'Excuse me, can you direct us to the seafront?' Stan asked, in his best, posh voice.

'You what?'

'The seafront,' I repeated. 'We fancy a stroll along the prom.'

He looked us up and down before answering, 'Well you'll have a long walk, the nearest beach is twenty miles. Are you sure you're up to it?' He smirked.

'I'll have you know I served in the Royal Marines, long before you were born, young man!' Stan stood to attention. 'Twenty miles was nothing to me.'

'Ahh, but that was then...' His smile softened. 'How about we all take a stroll to Annie's tea shop instead. It's just around the corner, and they do wonderful cakes,' he added leaning in towards us conspiratorially.

He was right. Stan and I spent a pleasant morning revisiting the Lyon's corner teashops of our childhood, until our brief foray into freedom came to an abrupt end.

'Oh Stan... Doreen... You've had us so worried,' said Matron – a touch of ice in her voice. 'We've been looking everywhere for you.'

'This isn't going to end well,' I said to Stan, feeling the impending telling–off, just like in the old days when I used to bunk off school.

'Too right, Batman.'

The Fleeting Grandfather

MY FIRST THOUGHT WHEN I arrive at the church and there is not a black-clad mourner in sight, is that I must have the wrong time. Just to be sure, I try the door which is firmly locked. Surely a place like Surrington can't have more than one church. I check the details on my phone and look at the ivy clad information board leaning crazily against a tree trunk. St Matthews – not Holy Trinity! I scan the horizon for any other spires and towers but can see no evidence of another church. Trust Aunt Anna to make things difficult and have her funeral at the most out-of-the-way venue possible. 'I don't want to put you to any trouble. Something small will do me.' I sigh in frustration at my now-deceased aunt.

Having retreated to my car and Google maps, I locate the church on the other side of town. Engrossed in my phone, I haven't noticed a man approach the car. I look up just as he is about to knock on the window. Probably some do-gooder wanting to give me directions. I wind down the window with a crisp, 'Yes?'

'Could you help? My wife has had a fall and I can't get her up.'

I bite down the 'For God's sake!' hovering on my lips and get out of the car.

'She's over here.'

As we make our way through the graveyard's long grass, I thank God for my knee-high boots. The man is surprisingly agile for someone who must be at least seventy and I am out of breath by the time we reach his wife.

I can see at once that she is dead, but just to be sure, I check for a pulse.

'I'm so sorry Mr... There is nothing we can do for your wife.'

'Dobbs... Gerald.'

'I think we should call an ambulance.'

'Yes... yes... whatever you think.' He waves the practicalities of the situation aside with an irritable wave of his hand.

I move away to give Mr Dobbs...and myself...some space. Having made the call I hover, unsure what to do next. I look across at Gerald kneeling beside his dead wife. I look at the time on my phone – I have missed the funeral now, anyway. I resort to further practicalities. 'Gerald, is there anything I can do? Anyone I can call for you?'

'No. But could you help me make Iris a bit more comfortable?'

We lay her on her back and cover her with my long black coat. 'They shouldn't be too long,' I say, praying my desperation isn't too obvious.

I sit on a nearby tombstone, wondering whether the damp moss will stain my trousers. Gerald sits beside Iris, holding her hand.

I listen to the birds and distant traffic on the main road – life continuing, regardless of death. 'Had you been married for a long time?' I imagine them meeting as childhood sweethearts and celebrating their golden wedding anniversary surrounded by numerous children and grandchildren.

'Only a year. We didn't have much time together.'

'I'm so sorry.' My training as a pharmacist has not equipped me with the skills for such a conversation and I'm not sure of the next step, so I choose to stay silent.

'We met online. I wanted to meet someone young at heart – someone who hadn't allowed old age to defeat them – and I thought anyone who was online would be a good start. We hit it off straight away...'

I allow the silence to continue.

'Neither of us have been married before – both busy with our careers – and have only found time for marriage since we got to our seventies.'

I'm tempted to say something inane like, 'Goodness!' but resist.

'What a year we've had together! We've travelled to India (for her) and the Arctic (for me), we've hired a campervan and done a road trip around Scotland, we've eaten at the best restaurants and generally spent lots of money. Neither of us had grasping and disapproving children to contend with, and who needs money in old age if you've even one year of memories shared with someone you love, to look back on and relive?' The final sentence has the well-worn feel of something spoken many times.

'Thank you for giving me that year, Iris. Travel well.'

He draws my coat over her face and, with some difficulty, gets up. 'I think we should wait in your car. There's no point in me catching my death as well.' I smile inwardly, wondering if he is aware of the joke.

We have only been in the car for a few minutes when the ambulance arrives, and the business of despatching Iris is done briskly and reverently.

Gerald and I stand watching the ambulance disappear down the road. Having no idea of the social etiquette for such occasions, I turn to Gerald. 'It's nice to have met you.' Doesn't seem right, somehow. 'I'm so sorry,' is all I can manage. I fidget with the belt of my coat, waiting for some signal from Gerald as to what should happen next. Should I just say goodbye and go? He is still scanning the horizon as if Iris might have changed her mind and decided not to die after all. 'I just couldn't leave you, Gerald.'

I'm in uncharted waters.

Eventually Gerald heaves a sigh as turns to me. 'Thank you so much...'

'Clare,' I say, resisting the urge to shake hands. Even I know we are way past that stage. 'Clare Sweeting.'

'Well, I won't keep you.'

'It's no problem. The funeral will be over by now,' I say looking at my watch as if to confirm the fact. 'It was my aunt's. I came to the wrong church by mistake.'

'Oh.'

It dawns on me that Gerald is as much at a loss as I am about post-death etiquette. Would it seem inappropriate to suggest a drink? I know I could do with one, so I plunge in, regardless. 'I don't know about you, but I could do with a drink. I can see a pub over there.'

'Yes indeed. I think a brandy is definitely called for under the circumstances. Thank you.' In spite of, or may be because of his obvious relief at not being left alone, Gerald's shoulders droop, and he looks his age.

When we have both taken a steadying sip of our brandies the silence is broken by a simultaneous, 'What...?' 'How...?' We exchange a smile and Gerald gestures for me to speak.

'Were you visiting someone...a grave?'

'Yes and no. I've been doing some family history, and we were looking for my great-grandfather's grave.' Gerald takes another sip and places the glass carefully on the table, in the centre of the beer mat. I appreciate the precision of this action.

'It's something that becomes important somehow as you get older. When you've lived most of your life, it seems that you need to know where you've come from and how you fit into the grand scheme of things. Not being religious, it's a way for me to understand what meaning our brief lives have.' Gerald sits back in the chair and closes his eyes. 'Especially after this morning.'

'Did you find him?'

'My great-grandfather? No, we'd only just got there when...' he stares into the flickering fire and swallows. 'What about you? I'm guessing you're not from these parts if you came to the wrong church.'

'I live in London...' I pause, feeling that something more is required. 'I'm a pharmacist,' I add.

'And your aunt? Were you close?'

I'm not sure what Gerald means by 'close'. 'I'd not seen her for a few years, but we exchanged cards and wrote at Christmas.'

'Oh. Even so, I'm so sorry you missed the funeral. Won't your family be wondering where you are?'

I had been thinking the same thing but hadn't liked to get my phone out to check for messages. It hadn't seemed appropriate. But I took the opportunity now.

'Yes, probably. Would you excuse me if I check my phone?'

'Of course. Go ahead.'

Clare, where are you? You're usually the first to arrive at anything!

Followed by:

Getting worried, Sis. Where are you? It's just about to start!

And then:

Really worried. Where are you? Ring me!

'Gerald, would you mind if I step outside to ring my brother? You're right. He's worried.

'Of course. Go ahead.'

'Rich, it's me. I'm okay. I just got...delayed.'

I explain about Gerald and Iris. 'So you're holed up in a pub with some old guy?'

'I couldn't just leave him, Rich!'

'No, it's okay. I get it. Just teasing. Are you alright though?'

'I'm fine. How was the funeral?'

'Very Aunt Annie. Understated but with the maximum of fuss!'

We share a laugh.

'Say goodbye to her from me. Rich, can we meet at the old place for a drink tomorrow?'

'Sure. See you then.'

I return to Gerald except that Gerald's chair is empty. Assuming he's in the Gents, I finish my brandy and wait. After fifteen minutes I wonder where he is, and ask at the bar. 'Oh, he went out the back way while you were outside. Said to say thank you for your help.' The buxom landlady continues vigorously polishing glasses as she speaks. I rush outside, but there is no sign of Gerald, and I realise I don't know which car was his, where he lives, or anything. I feel strangely betrayed.

On my way back to London, I convince myself that it's for the best. I'd probably never have seen him again, anyway. This way saved an awkward goodbye, and the inevitable 'Let's keep in touch.'

The following evening is warm with early summer sun, and Rich and I sip our drinks by the canal. A rowdy group of football supporters make conversation almost impossible, and I'm wondering why we haven't gone somewhere quieter. Rich knows that I hate noisy places, but he seems oblivious, lost in a world of his own – in the sunlight dancing on the water. But this is not like him, so I grit my teeth and try to block out the noise with some deep breathing.

Eventually the fans decide to head for the next pub, and we are left in peace. I wait for Rich to speak, but he says nothing.

'Rich, what is it? What's wrong?'

He puts his head in his hands pulling his fingers through the thick black curls that our mother used to adore. 'It's... I don't know... I don't know what to do.'

I feel a prickle of alarm. This isn't the laid-back, carefree Rich I'm used to.

'Rich. What is it?' I try to hide the panic in my voice.

'Kerry has thrown me out. When we got back last night.'

'What? Why?'

I feel a sudden spurt of anger towards the sister-in-law who has robbed me of my brother for the last few years. Who does she think she is, sitting on her phone all day, while Rich grafts long hours at the hospital to keep her high-maintenance life afloat?

'It's my fault. I had a bit of a fling at work.'

'Oh my God. Rich!'

'It was nothing, but she found out.'

'You can stay at mine until you two sort things out.' I pat his arm awkwardly. 'It'll be like the old days.' I can't resist a smile, but Rich bursts into an embarrassing bout of crying.

'Come on, let's get you home.' I'm aware of hostile stares already coming my way from the other drinkers.

Somehow, I get him out of the pub, and we manage the short walk back to my flat.

Over the summer, I enjoy my rekindled bond with Rich. Yes, he makes the flat look untidy and he never puts things away, but I can forgive him for that because I'm so glad to have him back – all to myself. When I'm with Rich, the little things don't seem to matter as much.

One evening, he comes home from another long shift and falls exhausted into his favourite chair. We've almost become an old married couple, with our own chairs – set in our ways. I love it.

'I had a patient today asking if I have a sister called Clare. Can you believe it?'

'Really?' I frown. My social circle is small – just people at work really, and I immediately think the worst. Someone stalking me, or some kind of scam, maybe. 'What's he called?'

'Gerald something-or-other.'

I sit up and look at Rich. 'Gerald? An old guy?'

'Well, yes! Gerald is not exactly a young person's name, is it?' Rich takes a long swig from his can of beer.

'Is he still there?'

'I should thing so. He broke his hip in a fall so I had to do emergency surgery. I don't think he'll be going anywhere for a while.'

I stand up and start putting my jacket on.

'What...? Where are you going?'

'It's Gerald! You know, from the day of the funeral.'

'The old guy from the pub?'

'I think so. I need to go and see. Do you think they'll let me in?'

'Just say you're his granddaughter or something. They'll let family members in. You might need to be forceful though.' Rich grins slyly at me. He knows I can do 'forceful' when I need to.

I arrive at Reception and ask for Gerald Dobbs in my most commanding voice, announcing myself as his granddaughter. The woman laconically examines her screen, picks up the phone and converses with someone in a low voice, eyeing me with hostility. Eventually, with some disappointment in her voice, she says, 'You can go up. Euston Ward. Third floor.'

I don't recognise the man in the corner bed, by the window. Gerald seems to have become a shrunken, paler version of the man I had met a few months before.

He recognises me, immediately. 'Hello, Grand-daughter,' he says, a twinkle in his eye. 'So Dr Sweeting is your brother. It's such an unusual name, and I thought of you immediately.'

'Yes, he mentioned you had asked about me, and I knew it must be you. I don't know any other Geralds,' I add by way of explanation.

He smiles. Thank you so much for coming, Clare. It seems you are turning into my guardian angel – always there when I need help.

I turn away to find a chair and hide my embarrassment, returning to sit beside the bed. 'How are you feeling?

'Not too bad. Although, I'm thinking that the good times are well and truly over now. It's getting to the stage where those memories are going to come into their own.'

'You don't know that. Plenty of people make a complete recovery after hip surgery.' Gerald looks out of the window. I try to soften my tone. 'Although I can understand why you feel like that now.'

'They're trying to find me convalescent care in a nursing home because I live on my own. Everyone knows that once you go into those places, you only come out in a box.'

I'm at a loss. What should I say? Somehow, I know that platitudes are not what Gerald wants to hear.

A few weeks later I visit Gerald at The Pines – there is not a pine tree in sight. I am now his official granddaughter, apparently. He looks better, but I can tell he has lost his spark. Even the 'Hello, Granddaughter!' joke seems to have palled.

'Make the most of your life, Clare. This comes to us all in the end.' He gestures around the utilitarian, semi-medical room.

'Maybe I could bring you something to read? Or a puzzle book or something.' As soon as the words leave my mouth, I regret them. Gerald gives me a steady look over the rims of his glasses. 'Maybe not the puzzle book, then.'

As I stand to leave, he takes my hand. I freeze, unsure how to respond. 'Don't be afraid to get close to people, Clare. Don't make the mistake I made – leaving it all to the last minute.'

I find myself bending to kiss his cheek. 'See you soon...Grandad.'

'Thank you.' On the journey home, I feel an unfamiliar warmth inside and only realise I'm smiling when the man opposite me smiles back. Fortunately, we are at my station, and I make a hurried exit from the train.

The following week I arrive to visit Gerald.

'Are you here to see Mr Dobbs?'

'Yes, I am.'

The woman behind the desk, whose badge tells me she is Janine, shifts her weight from one foot to the other. 'I'm afraid he's gone.'

'What? Gone where?'

'No. Sorry, I mean gone, as in *passed*.' She emphasises the word in strangely unsettling sibilant whisper.

I grip the counter to steady myself. 'He's dead?'

'Well, yes, although we prefer not to use that phrase here.' I detect an air of disapproval.

'What happened?'

'He just passed in his sleep, I'm afraid. We tried to ring you earlier,' she says defensively.

I don't know how to process the shock and time seems to stand still...until Janine breaks the spell.

'What arrangements would you like us to make?'

'Arrangements?'

'You're his granddaughter, aren't you? Down as his next of kin?'

Gerald's crematorium funeral as laid out in his meticulous instructions, was attended by five people: myself and Rich, a colleague from the solicitor's office where he had worked, the lady who had cleaned for him for forty years, sobbing into a handkerchief, and the vicar – who hadn't known him at all.

I miss him. But I've still got Rich...for now. Deep down, I know that eventually he will either get back with Kerry, or meet someone else. I aften think about Gerald's advice and one day I'll do something about it, but there's plenty of time.

Due for publication on https://www.fictiononthe web.co.uk/ 27 May 2022

Pass the Chips

'ARE YOU GOING TO eat those?'

I shake my head and pass the polystyrene tray to Simon. It's just as well he doesn't know me, otherwise he'd be saying, 'Try one more mouthful.' Or 'You need to look after yourself.' Or, even worse, 'Do it for me, Katie.' Accompanied by pleading eyes and maybe a tear.

As it is, he doesn't question and wolfs down the rest of my fish and chips. I watch him with wonder, and not a little envy, humming and nodding his head as he finishes the last few chips. 'You can't beat fish and chips by the sea,' he mumbles.

It is our first date – a walk along the beach – and I decide to tell him nothing about my dysfunctional relationship with food. He'll find out soon enough...if he sticks around. Dating always involves food, but I've cleared the first hurdle by avoiding any need for plates and cutlery. *Good move, Katie.*

'I love this kind of food – I guess you'd call it street food – where you don't have to sit down, when you're not trapped by the tables and chairs. I like eating while you can interact with people and places. What do you think?' Simon turns to look at me. 'Sorry, I'm burbling on. Nerves probably.'

'Me too...I mean...this kind of food.' I hope I sound nonchalant. Maybe this could work.

We walk further. I want to find out more about Simon. 'You don't sound as if you come from round here.'

'No, I'm from Manchester originally, but I've been in Cornwall for a couple of years now. What about you?'

'I've always lived here. My ancestors were tin miners – I come from a small gene pool.'

Another few steps. 'What brought you here?'

'I'm a chef.'

I turn and walk back to the car.

The Power of Freedom

THE EARLY MORNING SUN reflected off the carriages of the departing train, and I felt that something of me was leaving with it. I watched as it disappeared around the bend and listened until the rackety sound had disappeared into the distance.

Sighing, I picked up my duffel bag and guitar and headed for the station concourse. The morning rush hour was getting into full swing and everyone seemed to have somewhere they needed to be in a hurry – except me. I had nowhere I needed to be and I wasn't in any hurry. Was this what freedom felt like?

For the the first time I was truly on my own and responsible for my own life. The security of my family had disappeared with the train, taking my parents and sisters to a new life down south. They had accepted my decision not to go with them, but I

116

knew they weren't happy. Susie, my twin sister, had been particularly vocal about me letting her down, and 'dumping her on Mum and Dad,' as she put it. But I had stood firm and now here I was – free. The plan was to take up my place at the music academy and stay with my aunt and uncle – all my stuff was already at their house – but something inside me wanted to explore this freedom a little more. I had everything I needed with me, including my guitar, and my fantasy of busking, always in the back of my mind, could now become a reality, maybe in the next few minutes.

I knew that a licence was required to busk on the concourse so I headed outside into the busy Tuesday morning. I wandered about until I found what looked like a good spot, close to a coffee shop – always a good thing – and heart thumping, tuned my guitar. Not having an amp, it soon became apparent that my music was lost in the general cacophony of city sounds, and most of the people rushing past didn't even notice me, never mind my music. Time to rethink.

Not having any money to buy an amp – where would I even get one in this part of the city? – I headed to a quieter spot in the park. There were still plenty of people about, but they weren't rushing around, just strolling or sitting on benches. I stayed well away from the kid's play area – I really didn't want to go there! I also ignored the occasional runner, ear buds firmly protecting them from the real world. I retuned the guitar and got started with some Satie to calm myself down. Soon I was lost in my own world, and was surprised by the sound of applause as I finished.

I opened my eyes to find an audience seated on the nearby benches, clapping enthusiastically. An elderly man, obviously their unofficial spokesperson, stood up. 'Thank you, young lady. You have given us so much enjoyment this morning.' There was much nodding and a general murmur of agreement. 'It's so refreshing to hear the classical guitar repertoire played by such a talented performer.'

I closed my mouth, embarrassed at my childishness. 'Okay, well, thank you so much.' There was an expectant pause as they waited for me to say more. 'Well, it's amazing to have such a lovely audience. I clapped awkwardly in their direction.'

'Are you done, or are you planning to play some more?'

'Well, um, how about some Vivaldi?' I had nowhere to be, and suddenly I really wanted to entertain these people.

There was more appreciative nodding as my audience settled themselves on their benches.

For the next hour we experienced Vivaldi, Bach, more Satie, and even some Brouwer.

When I eventually ran out of steam, I felt an adrenaline high coursing through my body. For the first time, I had been in control of my own performance – I'd played whatever I wanted, however I wanted. No worrying about an adjudicator or judging panel, or passing an exam, and the experience of such freedom was heady.

As the applause subsided and I gave an awkward bow, the elderly gentlemen rose to his feet. 'I think I can say for all of us,' he gestured around with his arm, 'that we are truly privileged to have enjoyed an unexpected concert this morning. Thank you.'

Looking around, I noticed that my audience had almost doubled in size and some were even standing.

As I was packing my guitar away, the older man approached me. 'I'm Jim,' he said, 'holding out his hand.'

I shook it. It felt strangely old-fashioned, but in a nice way. 'Alice,' I replied.

'Alice, could we find a way to make these concerts a regular event? We could club together and pay you,' he added hastily, noticing my hesitation. 'There are quite a gang of us who gather in the park of a morning. It breaks the day up for us, and gets us out of our houses, and we would love to hear more of your music.'

I took a breath and held it while I thought.

The morning concert in the park became a thing, once a week, and I found a way to fit it around my academy studies. In the winter, we moved into the nearby library, and as time went by, some of my newfound friends came and performed with me. The pain of my lost baby soon receded to a bearable level as I found myself helping many others escape their own losses and problems for an hour or so.

When I look back on my career, those people in the park were the most important audience I ever had.

Originally Published in *Secret Attic Booklet #18* October 2021

Holiday Nightmare

NINA SIGHED IN EXASPERATION.

'David, what are you doing?' When there was no response, she tried again. 'David! I only sent you in to get some beers, how difficult can it be?'

David slowly withdrew his head from the fridge and straightened his body to its full height.

'Well, I...'

'Oh for God's sake, people are waiting! It's not as if we entertain much as it is.'

Nina strode forward, pushing David out of the way. 'Move! I'll get them myself!'

She grabbed several packs, slammed the fridge door and headed back out to the wrap-around terrace that was imprisoning him for the duration of this two-week holiday. There was no escape from the apartment, and Nina, wanting to show off their seafront 'home from home,' had invited several of their holiday neighbours over for Sunday afternoon drinks.

Sent in for more beers, David had stood, leaning into the fridge, enjoying the cool and a few precious moments to himself. He had been desperately trying to convince himself for some time now that the way Nina treated him was okay. She had endured a lot of emotional trauma in her past, so it wasn't her fault really, was it?

At home, things were at least bearable, as they were both at work during the day and Nina spent a lot of evenings out with 'the girls' doing God-knows-what. But David didn't really care as it meant he had the house to himself and could listen to his beloved Mozart at full-blast – it wasn't the same through headphones.

But this holiday, where they were imprisoned 24/7 was testing David to his limits. Nina didn't like sight-seeing or walking, content to lie on the sun lounger all day, gossiping with her new best friends. That wouldn't have been too bad if David had been allowed to go out on his own and explore, but Nina expected him to be at her beck and call at all times. 'For God's sake, David, no one else's husband wanders off on their own on holiday. It's a time for us to be together.' This has been accompanied by a flirtatious wink, which had triggered a familiar sense of panic in David. He knew how this Sunday afternoon drinks session would play out. Nina would get drunk and insist they head for the bedroom and David's ultimate nightmare would begin all over again, the session ending with the usual shouting, tears and recriminations.

Suddenly, David knew he could not deal with another of these scenes, however much he felt sorry for Nina. He felt a cold, visceral anger start to take seed deep inside him and knew he had to get away – now.

He strode into the bedroom, changed into a pair of trousers, grabbed his wallet, phone and car keys, and left.

A few hours and many missed calls from Nina later, David found himself enjoying a beer in a beach bar fifty miles further along the coast. As he drove along the coast road, the anger that had taken root grew and grew, and David knew that things could never go back to the way they were.

Nina's patience with David had worn thin long ago; he was so pathetic. He never stood up for himself; he wasn't even really a proper man. She wondered why she stayed with him, but deep down, she knew the reasons: money and security. Her childhood had been a series of late-night flits, her hapless parents permanently on the verge of eviction. Nina had hated that rootless existence and determined at an early age that her life was going to be very different.

She couldn't believe her luck when, at just nineteen, she met David, a trainee solicitor, well able to give Nina the security she craved. Everything had been just as she wanted it for the first few years. David adored her and had encouraged her to continue her training as a beauty therapist; she enjoyed being around other women, gossiping about the latest celebrity scandal. Nina knew she still needed David to maintain the lifestyle she'd always wanted, but, God, he was annoying, and as for their sex life ...the less said about that the better!

A while after she had returned to her guests armed with the drinks – he couldn't even do that properly! – Nina became aware that David hadn't reappeared, but she was enjoying herself too much to worry. Let him sulk. It was more fun without him anyway. After a while her new friends picked up on the fact that David hadn't reappeared.

'Oh, he's just had to deal with a work thing,' she said, inwardly seething.

When everyone had gone, Nina staggered around the apartment looking for David, and, eventually, through a drunken haze, realised he'd gone...and taken the rental car. She tried ringing him over and over, her fury growing.

David knew that he had to return to the apartment if only to get his passport, but he also knew that it was time to face facts…and Nina, and admit the relationship was over. Now that his anger had been recognised and unleashed he knew that the marriage would become even more toxic.

He drove back, braced for the inevitable onslaught, but was greeted by an astonishingly contrite and apologetic Nina.

'I'm so sorry, David. I've been such a bitch. I promise things will change from now on. Look, I've poured some of your favourite red wine and even found some Mozart for you. Let's talk and sort stuff out.'

As he became aware of the music flooding the room, David was speechless; this wasn't how he'd imagined this playing out. He allowed himself to succumb to this new Nina as she led him to the sofa.

'Cheers. To us,' said Nina as they clinked glasses.

'Cheers. Look… Nina, things have got to change—'

'They will, babe, I promise.'

As David slipped into unconsciousness, he realised he should have known that Nina would always get her own way.

Originally published in *Secret Attic Booklet #17* June 2021

A Shipwreck of Memories

This story was written in response to a black and white photo of a boy in swimming trunks, with his back to us, looking at the skeleton of a shipwreck.

IN MY DREAMS I am still that eight-year-old boy, standing on the beach, staring at the image of the wreck. And although I am undressed for the beach, in my swimming trunks, it is never summer.

My eight-year-old self feels isolated and vulnerable, although I don't know those words yet. I just want to go home to the safety of my mother – except that my mother is not safe, and neither is my home.

The dream always ends the same way. I am stuck in the mud and can't move, slowly being sucked down – sinking into oblivion. The last thing I see is the crazy outline of the shipwreck floating in the sky above me before my eyes fill with mud.

And then I wake up, gasping for air, thrashing my arms and legs about to make sure that I can still move.

The therapist says that the dream means that I feel my life is a wreck, and that I feel isolated and vulnerable, that the little boy in me wants to run home to some kind of soft, soothing mother figure. 'It's okay you're safe now, it was just a dream.'

She's right, my life is a wreck. Although you wouldn't know it from outward appearances. I am 'happily married', I have three children, I am a wealthy barrister, and yet – the little eight-year-old me still keeps returning to haunt me in my dreams.

'What can I do to stop these dreams?'

'Well, it seems to me that you need to sort your life out, and get rid of the wreckage.'

'I really don't know where to start, because the wreckage is everywhere – although well hidden.' I give a wry smile. Did I just say that out loud?

'Start at the beginning. What is going on with your eight-year-old self?'

I close my eyes, pinch the bridge of my nose and take a deep breath. Can I really go back there?

'It started when I was eight – after my father died. My mother changed into a different person;

someone who didn't seem to notice me anymore. I didn't know why. And then she started bringing men home, late at night. I didn't know who they were but there was often a lot of shouting, screaming, and other noises that I tried to block out with the pillow over my head.'

I shift in my chair, crossing one leg over the other. Here it comes... Will I be able to say it?

'Sometimes they were still there in the morning when I was getting ready for school, and my mother said whoever it was, was my uncle Tony, Max, Peter... I can't remember all the names. But I do remember one – he was called Ralph.'

I lean forward, elbows on my knees, and put my head in my hands. I can't look up.

'Ralph was there a lot, and he and my mother used to wake me up. He told her it would be good for me – it would make me a man. He always made her leave the room. I didn't know... I didn't know that this wasn't supposed to happen. All I knew was that I hated it, and I hated Ralph, and most of all I hated my mother.'

I am shocked at the tears running down my face, and my whole body is shaking. There is a silence while I try to recover myself. I don't know how long it lasts because time doesn't exist in my past life.

Eventually, I sit up.

'How long did this go on for?' I sense a gentleness in her voice which brings on a fresh bout of undignified crying, and I can't control the sounds I am making. Then there is another silence.

'Two years.'

'And then?'

'And then it just stopped and he never came back. I don't know why. My mother just said it was none of my business. But it was my business.' I can feel anger growing.

'And you never told anyone?'

'No. By the time I was old enough to know it shouldn't have happened, it was too late. It was too embarrassing – too humiliating. I just locked it away in a box in the very back of my mind.'

'But you haven't really locked it away, have you? It's there all the time.'

'I don't know what to do with it.'

'You've taken the first step. It will take courage to open the box completely and examine what is inside, but that is the journey you must take to escape from your past.'

I look out of the window and through my adult eyes I see it is raining. The weather has come out in sympathy with my tears. Suddenly, I need to move. I stand up and walk a few paces to and fro, relieved that I am not trapped in the past, shrouded in the sand, knowing that I am my adult self who can be in control of my own safety, and that I can create a better world for myself. I am no longer a small child at the mercy of the very people who should have kept me safe.

Many gruelling sessions later, I came to several conclusions: one, I had married the wrong woman. (I'd been looking for a substitute mother-comforter figure, something that she didn't want to be – understandably); two, I owed it to my children to get better; three, I wanted to teach them to be courageous and always face things however difficult and embarrassing; four, I loved my job and wanted to use my skills to make sure that the Ralphs of this world would never see the light of day once I'd finished with them.

I've not had the dream for two years, and my eight-year-old self is now peaceful, understood and comforted.

Originally published in *Secret Attic Booklet #24* – Picture This! winner

Finding the Real Peter

HOW HAD IT COME to this? Peter buried his face in his napkin and sobbed, oblivious to the other diners in The Golden Fleece, next to the Premier Inn on the ring road. This was not how he had imagined his career would end – an ignominious send-off with only his loyal secretary, Pat, for company; and even she had left, having barely sipped her wine, muttering something about getting home to her mother. Even so, he put a brave face on things and ordered his meal. But as he raised the first forkful of food to his mouth, Peter saw himself – sitting in this anonymous restaurant with two Happy Retirement cards – one signed by everyone in the office and the other from Pat, alongside the Homebase gardening voucher in his wallet. In his imagination, he would have held his leaving do in the swanky Yodo restaurant in town, with the whole department toasting his wonderful career, and wishing him and Anna a wonderful retirement in their French villa.

Peter left a twenty pound note on the table, and strode out of the restaurant. He got into his Lexus and headed for the motorway. He might as well enjoy one more journey, as it was being repossessed tomorrow.

It was difficult to know exactly when things had gone wrong. Was it the morning he'd needed a drink before going to work? Was it the day when his hands shook so badly that he'd had to leave a junior surgeon to finish up? Maybe it was as far back as the first time he had drunk a bottle of wine on his own. No wonder Pat couldn't bring herself to share a bottle of wine with him. What had he been thinking? It had been the final, pathetic, flimsy, attempt to pretend that things were normal.

As he drove, Peter's thoughts turned back to the life he'd had ten years ago – when he'd had it all. A brilliant cardio-thoracic surgeon, pioneer of cutting– edge techniques, highly respected by his colleagues and on the board of the hospital. He saw himself coming home from work and joining Heather in decorating the house with their two children, home from university for Christmas, laughing at the usual family jokes as they planned their annual summer holiday together in the St Tropez villa. But somehow, there had come a time when having it all had not been enough, and Peter had found himself, in his early fifties, thinking, *What else is there?* In those days, no one talked about mental health, or depression. Most people wouldn't have even recognised the symptoms – not even a medical professional like Peter; or maybe, *especially* a medical professional like Peter.

He and Heather had got into the habit of drinking a bottle of wine each evening 'to unwind,' after the younger of their children had left for university. Then, one evening, Heather had been visiting her parents and Peter, unable to break the habit, had drunk a bottle of wine on his own. From there, slowly but surely, over the next ten years, alcoholism had stealthily crept up on him. Things had come to a head when, one day, a junior doctor had alerted the CEO that he could smell alcohol on Mr Walker and didn't think he was fit to operate. Peter had never stepped into an operating theatre since, as arrogantly and obstinately he refused help and refused to even to acknowledge the problem, insisting that other colleagues were 'out to get him.' Left with no other option, the hospital had insisted on immediate early retirement with a reduced pension. And so it had come to this: even now, refusing to accept that a demon was running his life, even ordering a bottle of wine this evening, and expecting Pat to drink it with him. What had he been thinking? In fact, what had he been thinking for the last year or so?

Heather, finding out from a friend at the hospital, had immediately moved out and was currently taking him to the cleaners, intent on bleeding him dry. The legal fees alone, would wipe him out. His children weren't talking to him, and he knew that he would have to leave the area. The hospital had hoped to hush things up but, inevitably, the local press had got wind of the scandal, and his face had been in every paper.

Peter found that he had driven almost all the way to Leeds. This was the first evening he could remember not having a drink; somehow he hadn't been able to face it after Pat had left. He felt himself to be at a fork in the road: he could turn off at the next exit and return home and get help, or he could drive on into oblivion, allowing his pride, self-pity and anger to overwhelm him.

Three weeks later, Peter found himself dressed in uncharacteristic jogging bottoms and a T-shirt, running along a beach. 'Come on. Keep going, old man,' shouted Tim over his shoulder as he sprinted off. Peter stopped, hands on his knees, struggling to get his breath. He had not felt this good in a long time.

Tim returned and patted him on the back. 'You're doing great, Dad – for an oldie.'

'Do you know, Tim, I never thought I could feel this good with so little,' he puffed.

'I'm so proud of you, Dad. Mum and Lizzie will come round, eventually, you know.'

'I know this sounds a bit soft, but I think I'm only now getting to know the real Peter – who I really am.'

'Me too. And I think I'm going to like him...a lot. Come on, let's get you a latte and boost your sugar levels. Race you!' And he was gone.

Originally published as *The Real Peter* in *Secret Attic Booklet #15* June 2021

Lost and Found

Having lived in the wonderful city of Norwich for twenty-five years, I couldn't resist setting one of my stories there.

MARNIE KNEW FOR CERTAIN that she was a bad mother the day she lost Archie. One minute she'd been browsing through the second-hand books on Sam's market stall, safe in the knowledge that Archie was beside her making a fuss of Sam's dog, Bess, and the next, she was in a state of panic overlaid with a thin veneer of 'Don't worry, he's around here somewhere.'

But after twenty minutes of Marnie and Sam searching and calling down every aisle of the covered market, her panic broke through. The traders on Norwich market were a close-knit bunch and word travelled fast, but in spite of all their efforts,

Archie had vanished. Marnie felt her fragile world imploding as she collapsed into a wailing heap. By this time Sam had alerted the two PCSOs patrolling nearby, and while one was busy talking on the radio, the other was doing her best to comfort Marnie: 'He can't have gone far, love. Don't worry, we'll find him.'

But Marnie knew that it was too late. Now everyone would know what she'd known inside for a long time – she was a bad mother. Georgie had said it often enough, after her first bout of post-natal depression, and again after her second breakdown when Archie was three and she had apparently walked out of the house leaving him alone, sleeping in his bed. Marnie had no recollection of anything about that night until she had come-to on the secure ward at Hellesdon. Although she loved Archie with a force that took her breath away, Marnie knew he deserved better. Just as Georgie had always said.

In defeat, she felt the energy leave her body. She could feel herself falling – as lost as the unknown river flowing nearby. The black water silently beckoned her, as it had done the last time she'd lost herself. Nothing had any meaning any more.

'Come on, Marnie. Don't give up. You have to fight to find Archie – he's your son.' Sam was crouching, eye-to-eye with her, and Marnie felt his desperation to drag her back from oblivion.

She put her head in her hands and closed her eyes, as usual, retreating from a situation that was too much to handle. Returning to the safety of the dark river. Was this how she was going to live the rest of her life, running away from every challenge?

And then something clicked in her head: *Whether I'm a good mother or not, **he is my son**! Nothing can change that...ever. If I don't do something now, I'll never be able to live with myself.*

Marnie felt some of her energy return as the power of the river receded. She straightened her back, lifted her head and jumped to her feet.

'I need to find him!' She impatiently shook off the arm that Sam had put around her shoulders

'Okay, is there anywhere around the market or nearby that he likes to go?' The PCSO had become more business-like. Marnie saw from her badge that she was called Hayley.

Marnie was tempted to reply, self-pityingly that she wouldn't know because she only had access to Archie every other weekend, and that only recently had those visits been unsupervised. But she caught herself. 'He is your son.' She chanted the mantra inside her head.

She thought. 'Well, I know he likes Langleys, the toy shop in the arcade.'

'Okay. Walk with me and we'll see if we can find him. Sam, you stay here in case Archie comes back.' Hayley then nodded to her colleague who was on the radio.

They walked along a stall-lined alley, heading for the toy shop. Marnie looked left and right down each alley that ran across at right-angles, frantically searching for Archie's red T-shirt and mop of blond, curly hair. How could he have just vanished? He must be here somewhere. Marnie's need to find him was now all-consuming and her focus was razor-sharp.

They reached the end of the market and searched up and down Gentleman's Walk, Marnie showing passers-by a picture of Archie on her phone.

'Can you send me that? I'll get it distributed,' said Hayley.

Marnie did as Hayley asked, reluctant to take her eyes away from her surroundings, even for a moment.

'Okay, let's head in to Langley's, my colleagues have got this area covered now.

Today, Marnie was oblivious to the welcome cool of the Royal Arcade on a hot day – her sole aim was to get to the toy shop.

'You look upstairs, I'll search down here,' Hayley ordered.

Marnie rushed up the stairs, taking them two at a time. Her frantic search, which took all of one minute, was fruitless. She returned to Hayley who shook her head. None of the staff had seen Archie.

'It's pretty certain that he hasn't been in here. Do you think he could have found his way to the Jarrold's toy department?' Hayley's calm was starting to get to Marnie. Her heart was thumping and a terrible sense of dread was growing with each minute. Without answering, Marnie set off at a sprint towards Jarrolds. Once inside, she climbed impatiently up the snail-paced escalators, pushing people aside with no time or thought for apology.

She raced past the cuddly toys and colouring books, and there he was!

Archie was looking at a box of Lego, Georgie crouching beside him.

'Mummy! Look what Daddy's getting me.' Archie ran forwards grabbing Marnie's hand to drag her over, but Marnie just took him in her arms and held him tight, sobbing with relief.

After a few moments, Archie wriggled free and looked uncertainly at Marnie, and then at Georgie. 'Why is Mummy crying?'

'I think Mummy thought she'd lost you,' said Georgie giving Marnie a smug grin.

Marnie ignored him and turned to Archie, crouching down to speak to him. 'Archie, you must never, never wander off when we're out.'

'I didn't. Daddy just went like this.' Archie did a beckoning motion with his hand. 'And he did this.' Archie put his finger to his lips. 'Just like in school when we have to be quiet and not say anything. It was Daddy so I knew it was okay,' he continued earnestly.

Marnie held his arms and looked into his eyes. Even if it's Daddy, you mustn't go off without telling me. I have been so worried. She saw understanding dawn in his eyes which soon filled with tears.

'I'm sorry, Mummy.'

'It's okay now. I'm happy now I know you're safe. Go and sort out your Lego, and I'll see you when Daddy brings you home later.' She gave Archie a final hug and gave Georgie a long, angry stare.

Just at that moment, Hayley arrived.

'I've found him. He was with his father.' Marnie was so consumed with anger she found it hard to get the words out.

Hayley seemed to assess the situation. 'Is Archie staying with his father?'

'Yes, for the rest of the afternoon, and he's bringing him home later, isn't that right, Georgie?'

'Yup. I guess Marnie needs to take one of her tranquilisers and lie down for a bit after this fiasco,' he sneered, putting his arm protectively around Archie.

'Right. Marnie, let's get a coffee and have a chat.' Although she sounded her usual, detached self, Marnie noticed an element of sympathy in Hayley's voice. She spoke into her radio, calling off the search as they headed out of the department store to the nearest coffee shop.

Once they were walking along with two takeout coffees, Hayley said, 'So, can you fill me in on what just happened back there?'

Marnie was amazed at how cool-headed she felt. This wasn't about her, it was about Archie, and for the moment he was safe and happy, that was all that mattered.

She told the story of the last five years, and between sips of coffee, Hayley listened intently.

'So, are you telling me that Georgie deliberately lured Archie away to make it look as if you weren't capable of looking after him properly?' There was a tinge of anger in Hayley's voice.

'I know it seems bonkers, but yes, that's exactly what I'm telling you,' said Marnie firmly.

'Not as bonkers as you think. In this job, I've seen people do all sorts of things to get their own way. We'll be questioning Georgie about this, and possibly charging him with wasting police resources.' Hayley paused. 'And I suggest you get some legal advice,' she added, firmly.

When Georgie returned Archie later that afternoon, Marie refused to make eye contact, closing the door firmly as soon as the goodbyes had been said.

Once Archie was settled in bed, Marnie sat with a glass of wine and reflected on what had happened. Something had caused a monumental shift in her thinking, and she had seen a glimpse of the old, pre-Archie, Marnie. She thought back...

She and Georgie had met in the Student's Union bar at the UEA where Marnie had been finishing her Geography MA on the lost rivers of Norwich. It was a subject that held endless fascination – how did a river vanish, or become 'lost'? Sipping her wine, Marnie thought again of the Great Cockey that had once flowed in full view near the bustling market where events had unfolded earlier. But in that moment, Archie, the Great Cockey and Marnie herself, had all disappeared from view – lost to the bustling crowds around them.

She had been lost, in a dark, underground place for five years. But today was the day that she had found herself, as well as Archie. Somehow, a strength had come to her enabling her to face anything and anybody – even Georgie, if it meant that Archie was safe. That she was a mother, good, bad or indifferent. Marnie realised that she had heard what Sam said – really heard, and she had stopped judging herself – making everything about the weak, needy, Marnie, who was trying to prove...what? That she was worthy of Archie?

No more! Things were different now – she didn't have to prove her worthiness to Georgie or anyone else. She was Archie's mother, and always would be.

Six months later, Marnie sat in the school hall, watching Archie play an angel in the Christmas play, feeling as if her heart would burst with pride. Miss Webster had cast Archie well – with his blond curls and clear singing voice, he was every bit an angel.

Now that he was living full-time with Marnie, she had learnt that he wasn't always an angel in real life, but she had got to know the sensitive, caring, sometimes boisterous and demanding little individual, that was Archie.

Marnie had taken Hayley's advice, and once Georgie realised that Marnie had 'lawyered up' as he put it, his arrogance and emotional manipulation shrank and disappeared like the air from a punctured balloon. Within a few months, following a few letters from Marnie's solicitor, he had meekly agreed that Archie should live with her, and that he would have access at the weekends. Lately, however, it seemed that he had a new, pregnant, girlfriend and the visits had become sporadic. Marnie had wondered if she should warn this girl about what lay in store for her, but decided against it, thinking that the girl would probably think of her as the 'bitter ex.' She knew instinctively that's what Georgie would be saying.

Now that Archie was at school, she had been able to indulge her fascination with the hidden history of Norwich, and was now employed as a guide for walking tours around her beloved city. Now that Marnie was no longer lost, she had ideas for a book about lost rivers. She could already envisage the chapter titles in her head.

Originally published on https://cafelit.co.uk 24 November 2021

Memories

ISSY PICKED HER WAY through the shallow water, revelling in the warmth and the sand between her toes. She couldn't resist the habit of always being on the lookout for perfect, undamaged shells – she loved to paint and draw them, recording their detail and beauty. Trips to the beach on warm, sunny afternoons like this didn't happen very often these days and she was determined to make the most of this one. From the corner of her eye she saw a small boy and his father working industriously on a complex sand castle – a model of something in the father's mind, maybe? Issy studied them covertly as she continued walking and wondered whether they were enjoying every moment of this perfect day and preserving the memories in some mental larder, to be taken out and enjoyed when harder times came...as inevitably they would.

Her thoughts were disturbed by a frantic shouting and waving further down the beach. Heaving a sigh,

Issy picked up her pace and broke into a half-run towards Toby.

'Mum, mum, something's happening to Dad and I don't know what to do,' her son gasped as she drew nearer.

'It's okay, Toby, I'm sure he'll be fine. I'm sorry to have left you for so long.' She rushed over to where John was bent over in his wheelchair. 'I've got you, John. Just breathe. It's all right, I'm here.' She held him as the spasm passed. When she was sure he could breathe evenly again, she gave him a drink from the lidded cup that went with them on their increasingly rare trips out.

'Mum, I'm so sorry, I just panicked. How do you manage all this?' he gestured vaguely towards his father. 'I think it's time we got you some help, or maybe he needs residential care. Donna and I could help with the finances.'

'Toby, while ever your father is aware of his surroundings and understands my presence, I need to be with him, to help him through this. Can you understand?'

'I know, and I do understand, but you're exhausted. Let us at least get some help in one day a week so you have time to do your painting, and recharge your batteries.'

Issy smiled at the cliché. Toby worked in a world of apps and internet technologies which seemed to have a language consisting of set phrases like: 'I got this,' 'Smell the coffee,' 'Blue sky thinking,' to name but a few she'd heard him using on the phone to people at work. She realised that he needed to do something, to feel useful and so agreed that they would look into it. And if she was honest, she often had visions of a whole day of painting with no interruptions or demands on her time.

'I guess it's time we got back,' she said to no one in particular. She couldn't resist a glimpse at the father-and-son project further back along the beach. Her rosy view of the creation of wonderful memories was abruptly shattered as she saw the boy kicking the carefully crafted structure apart in temper and frustration. She was too far away to see the father's face or hear what he was saying, but the way he threw his hands in the air and strode back to the family encampment, rage emanating from his whole body, said it all.

Real life had a habit of intruding on even the smallest fantasy sometimes, and Issy was suddenly grateful for the memories she had of the good times with John. The ecstasy and excitement that had made their early relationship special, when he had first become her lover. The special times with John and Toby – holidays and parties, and everyday events – she treasured them all, and they sustained her now as the John she knew was gradually slipping from her grasp.

'Ready, Mum?' Issy sensed that Toby was anxious to get back to his life of computers and technology, where he felt safe.

'Yep,' let's go home.

A Growing Community

ALISON PUT DOWN HER trowel and wiped the sweat from her forehead as she straightened her aching back. She glanced around at her fellow workers beavering away in various sections of the garden and smiled at the warmth she felt deep inside.

It hadn't always been like this. There had been many dark and difficult times during which Alison could have never imagined enjoying the outdoor life, never mind gardening! At her lowest point, avoiding the anti-depressants the GP prescribed, she had downloaded a meditation app and religiously kept to a fifteen-minute meditation every day. Following the disembodied advice, she had made it her sole target to get through the day. And, when she went to bed, if she could think of one good thing, she gave herself a bonus point.

It had been a long path out of depression and had taken Alison several gruelling weeks to stick to her resolution. As time passed, however, she found the list of good things getting longer at the end of each day, and a few things even made her smile. She learnt to take pleasure in a leaf falling to the ground, a flower growing in the wall along the street, or the sound of the busker by the shops. She stopped and looked. Really looked.

One of the things that grabbed her attention – how come she had never noticed it before? – was the unloved piece of land opposite her flat. The council came once or twice a year to clean up and stop it becoming a wilderness, but it was merely an expanse of something that resembled grass. Alison had seen a piece on the news about how an urban community had turned an unloved plot of land into a thriving community garden, and somehow the idea took root in her mind. She couldn't stop thinking about it.

After much procrastinating, Alison had put her legal skills into practise and persuaded the local council to allow her and some of her neighbours to make a garden on the wasteland. The real turning point had been when Alison hosted a meeting. In a leaflet explaining her plan, she invited all the residents in the block to meet in her flat. She had been on the point of cancelling several times when panic set in, but, somehow, she knew deep down, that if she didn't take this chance to start relating to people again, she would never truly escape from her life on this isolated island .

The only other person Alison knew in the block, Gheeta, next door, had been sceptical: 'You have got to be joking, Alison. Do you even know anything about gardening? Where are we going to get all the tools and plants from?'

But, in spite of some scepticism, the meeting had been special, and many residents had been grateful for the chance to get out of their flats and meet the people they shared their building with. It turned out that there was an epidemic of loneliness in the block. As the meeting progressed, it became apparent that the attendees had many talents, including Wanda, who had been a garden designer before she retired. Bruce, who worked in a local garden centre, was despatched to see if they would be prepared to donate some plants and equipment in return for a small plaque recognising their generosity.

The council, after much lobbying by Alison, eventually agreed to provide the workforce and machinery to clear the land and lay out the basic areas, as set out on Wanda's plan. 'Think how good it will look in the council magazine, and in your annual report,' Alison had pointed out.

During a brief lull in the heavy metal music of the council machinery pounding through her flat one morning, Alison became aware of a bird-like tapping on her door.

Hovering outside on the landing was a thin young woman, nervously rocking on her toes. Alison had passed her on the stairs a few times, but they had never spoken. 'Hi,' she said. She knew instinctively much it had cost the woman to knock on Alison's door.

Her visitor took a deep breath, and nervously tucked a strand of her long black hair behind her ear. 'Hi, um... I'm Annette. I got your leaflet about the garden and...' she paused, swallowing hard, 'and I noticed on the plans that you're having a pond and a wild area.' Annette avoided making eye contact, focusing on something behind Alison's shoulder

'Yes, we are. Is it something you're interested in? We don't really know what we're doing with it, just getting ideas off the internet really.'

Annette took a deep breath and clasped her hands together. 'Well, before I got ill with this...depression, I worked for the National Trust, restoring natural habitats, so I might be able to help.'

'Oh my God! That would be wonderful.'

'Really? Okay...well... Actually, I can't believe I've got out of my flat and just done this,' Annette said in a rush and met Alison's gaze for the first time. Some of the tension eased in her body as her shoulders dropped and she gave a sigh of relief.

'I know how much courage that took – I've been stranded in a dark place for the last couple of years, too. But this project has somehow got me out there and doing things. Things I used to be good at. So go for it, Annette! Why don't you jot down some ideas and come over for a coffee tomorrow? We can talk it through.'

The following day, Annette appeared with a notebook full of large, scrawly writing. 'I've been up half the night doing this. I haven't felt this alive in ages!' She took several nervous sips of coffee while Alison thumbed through the many pages.

'This is fantastic, Annette, and I love the idea of getting the local primary school involved. If we get everyone round, how would you feel about sharing these ideas with the gang?' Annette became very still, her hands clenched in her lap, and Alison was worried that she'd pushed her too far, too soon.

But she took a deep breath, and said decisively, 'Know what? Yes, I'll do it. What have I got to lose? Life can't get any worse than it's been the last few years.'

Alison gave her a warm smile. 'They'll be thrilled that you're going to be involved.'

One thing led to another and before Alison knew it, the garden was taking shape. Wanda's ambitious plans for the space which included flower beds, a vegetable garden with some raised beds, and Annette's designs for the pond area and the wildlife patch at the far end, complete with bug hotels and wood piles where nature could be left to its own devices, were gradually taking shape. 'What's a bloody bug hotel when it's at home?' Bill, an allotment veteran, had asked.

Apart from a few minor disagreements which were swiftly sorted out by a ruthlessly efficient committee chairperson in the form of Sonia, a retired headmistress, the community and the garden grew and thrived.

Bill was the go-to source for vegetable-related advice, and kept a strict eye on operations, while tending the raised beds from his wheelchair. Bruce managed to forage a surprising range of supplies from work, where a shocking number of plants were discarded because they 'weren't good enough to display.' Everything else they grew from seed, and after some training from Bill, Wanda and YouTube, window sills all over the block became mini plant nurseries.

Annette contacted the local primary school and arranged activities for the different classes that came on Wednesday mornings each week. Her enthusiasm was infectious and soon the children were excited about the changes they saw as the garden took shape, and the pond and wildlife area became home to a multitude of creatures. Annette, like the garden, blossomed and was soon unrecognisable from the anxious young woman who had knocked on Alison's door all those weeks ago.

Over the next few months, Alison became aware that nearly all the residents in the block were single – and many were retired. There were only a few couples, but they seemed too preoccupied with work and friends to pay much attention to the garden project. All that is, except Coral and Leroy, who, as time passed, became everyone's favourite mum and dad. Having run their own cafe for thirty years, they kept everyone working in the garden fed with a constant supply of mouth-watering Jamaican food, and Coral's weekend jerk chicken and fried plantain lunches were a highlight.

And so they became a family. Those who did not have traditional family to go to all gathered in Sonia's flat on Christmas Day for a real community feast featuring produce from the garden. Bill insisted on traditional sprouts and mashed swede, and of course, roast potatoes. Coral and Leroy pulled all the stops out with goat curry and Jamaican rum cake, and, Annette, her face beaming with pride had produced a Thai green curry, which her mother had taught her to make, giving step-by-step instructions from Thailand on Facetime. Those who could still move, roused themselves for charades and Guess Who I Am. Everyone agreed, it had been the best Christmas Day ever.

Alison felt herself coming back to life, as, day by day and week by week, she grew stronger, and the garden and her new family nurtured her. She knew that depression would always be lurking around the edges of her mind, and that she would have to be vigilant. But she knew the warning signs and had learnt strategies for dealing with them. Her friendship with Annette blossomed and she knew they would always be there to support one another, both understanding how truly frightening and debilitating a full-blown attack could be. Alison knew that she was content enjoying one day at a time, and that when the time was right, she would know when she was ready to branch out. But for now, this was just perfect.

Premonition

I RE-RUN THE DREAM in my head, pressing pause every so often to examine my thoughts. I need to be sure it is really me and not some other, fictional, dream person entering my sub-conscious.

How had I felt at the bus stop? Yes, this was me, anxious that the bus would be late, or worse still, not turn up at all. Was I talking to the woman who appeared with a buggy and a restless toddler? This wasn't me, so much. Anxiety about the child, jumping up and down, tugging at his mother's hand – definitely me. I see potential accidents at every turn.

I consider calling in sick and avoiding the whole incident, but if I don't go today, I will have to be there tomorrow, or the next day. I know I have to face the situation head-on, otherwise it will be in my head for ever, re-spooling on an endless loop.

The bus stop is deserted – a good start. I get through my familiar anxiety about the bus; so far so good. But then – is that a woman with a buggy and a toddler rushing along towards me? I want to run, but my premonition won't let me.

'I'm not too late for the number 29, am I?'

As she speaks the bus looms up behind her, the child breaking free of her hand. But I'm ready for this, I've rehearsed it. I leap forward and grab his coat.

Miss Pick's Lesson

'LOOK OUT, HERE SHE comes.'

We snigger and shuffle our feet.

Miss Pick strides along the corridor, a determined look on her face, but we are not fooled. We know the façade is only paper-thin.

We bide our time and walk demurely into the classroom, taking our seats in silence.

Miss Pick isn't fooled either – she knows something is up.

Swallowing loudly, she tells us that we are going to be learning about tectonic plates, and we resist the urge to laugh and call out 'prick' jokes.

The silence becomes oppressive and the tension builds as Miss Pick plunges on, through earthquakes and tsunamis.

Then at last Bella gives the signal, and all hell is let loose.

As one, we jump on our chairs – even on tables in the heat of the moment – and start shouting and screaming about an imaginary mouse.

Except things don't go as planned. The crash of Ben falling is lost in the chaos and only when Miss Pick hurtles herself forward do we realise that his unconscious body is on the floor.

'Move back!' There is a sudden authority in Miss Pick's voice, and we instinctively obey, returning shame-faced to the floor.

'Go and get help. Tell Mrs Brown to call an ambulance... Now!' she shouts at an ashen-faced George who is nearest the door.

We watch, trance-like as Miss Pick efficiently checks for vital signs and, undoing Ben's shirt, starts CPR. She mutters, 'Come on, Ben,' with each compression. Every so often she checks for a pulse. Suddenly, Ben takes a breath, and she kneels back, breathing hard, holding his hand.

The trance is broken as the medics arrive and we are ushered out of the room.

That day, Miss Pick taught us a lesson we would never forget.

Originally published in *Secret Attic Issue #28* April 2022

Lazy Days

SLOTH – RELUCTANCE TO work or make an effort. Idly clicking through the Seven Deadly Sins quiz on Facebook, Amy had made good progress until she reached Sloth. Her finger hovered...

Since lockdown everything had seemed a bit pointless. Days were spent flicking through social media and watching box sets. Did that count as Sloth? But that was what everyone was doing, wasn't it?

Amy felt irritated by this Sloth intruding into her lazy days. Now she couldn't get it out of her head!

Eventually Sloth generated some energy of its own, and Amy found herself clicking on Volunteer in Your Area on the council website.

Frozen in Time

CHLOE:

It was a freeze-frame, imprinted on my mind, never to be erased. The pre-kiss look between them. I was suddenly the third party, excluded from the intimacy of the moment.

My 'What shall we eat?' remained unasked. Instead, the 'What...?' hovered in the air between us.

Then motion returned as they pulled apart and looked at me.

'Sorry, Chloe. What was that?' Ewan leaned back in the chair, lazily crossing one leg over the other.

'What...was that?' I wanted to shout.

But, instead, in the moment, I affected an air of indifference, leaning idly against the door frame. 'What do you fancy to eat tonight?'

As soon as the sentence was spoken it was too late to go back. Normal service had resumed.

'It seems like a curry evening to me,' said Esther, giving Ewan a private look.

'Yup. Sounds good.' Ewan looked at me. 'Okay to order the usual?' he asked, eyebrows raised.

'I'll sort it. Delivery at eight?'

'Thanks, Chloe,' said Esther without looking at me.

Esther:

I thought we'd blown it this time. Surely Chloe must have seen – even *she* isn't that thick! How can she just carry on as if nothing happened? It seems that she's a throw-back to our mother's generation – sweep everything under the carpet and pretend it's not there. Avoid any awkward conversations and pretend everything is normal, and then it will be.

When she'd gone to order the takeaway, Ewan smiled, still leaning back in the chair. 'Well. What do we do now?'

'What do you mean, "What do we do now?"' I could feel my cheeks flushing with the anger resting heavy in my chest.

'She knows, but she's not going to say anything. Don't you think that's a bit weird? We can't just leave it at that.'

'I can't believe she's put us in this situation! Why couldn't she shout and fly off the handle like any normal person?' I could hear my voice turning into a shout. 'Now she's made things really awkward.'

Ewan:

I can't help enjoying watching Chloe and Esther driving each other mad. Really, they are more alike than they want to admit.

I didn't plan to bring things to a head tonight, but there, it just happened. Now, neither of them knows how to talk about what just occurred, and I can just sit back and watch the show – if there is one.

Maybe they'll both ignore the obvious and I'll be able to carry on seeing them both without anyone actually talking about it. A very French way of going about things. It quite appeals to me, but then I would never get the satisfaction of seeing them scratch each other's eyes out over me – which would be a shame.

Chloe:

I could hear Esther's voice from the kitchen while I was ordering the takeaway, but I resisted the urge to go and listen from the hall. Whatever they were arguing about, I wasn't going to get involved. In fact, I didn't know what I was going to do...about any of it.

The questions were beginning to trickle to the surface: How long? Why? And more importantly, how had I not known?

I closed my eyes and sat at the table where Esther and I had eaten thousands of meals, as toddlers, children, silent teenagers, and now as twenty-some-things clearing out our dead mother's belongings.

A very small part of me wondered whether Ewan was actually enjoying all this. He certainly hadn't seemed bothered; and come to think of it, it was only Esther's voice I heard, not Ewan's. There had been no shouting from him. And... Why hadn't I thought of this? Why hadn't he followed me to explain, grovel, and say it meant nothing – that it was just a fling. Wasn't that what people usually did? Why hadn't I made a scene? Forced them into some sort of apology? I banged my hands against my head in frustration.

Esther:

Even though I knew Chloe was seeing Ewan, it was obvious he was more interested in me once we'd met. One thing led to another and, before I knew it, six months had passed. I thought it was up to him to tell Chloe how things were – it was his relationship, not mine – she just happened to be my sister. And anyway, I hadn't wanted to force the issue.

But now, this evening, suddenly, I *do* want to force the issue. I want to know for sure that it is me he wants. But Chloe has ruined that by not saying anything. So now it is left to me to open the can and let the worms out. It is obvious that Ewan isn't going to do anything. What will happen if I come out with it? Will Ewan walked away from both of us? Or worse, choose Chloe. Unlikely as it is, it is still a possibility. And I can't take that risk.

Ewan:

I can see Esther's thoughts playing out in her restless hands and rounded shoulders. She doesn't have a clue how transparent she is. What will she decide? Will she go for a full-blown confrontation? Somehow, I think not. What will she do with all that simmering anger though? One of these days it will boil over. I hope I'm there to see when it does. I'm guessing that most of it will be directed at Chloe.

Poor Chloe; so trusting, just as needy as Esther in some ways. She lacks Esther's anger though – she's more accepting. Maybe that makes her the weaker of the two. We'll see, because I'm definitely sticking around to see how this plays out. Perhaps, in time, I can introduce a fourth party into the mix. That would be fun.

Originally published in *Secret Attic Booklet #19* October 2021

Better than Me?

'YOU THINK YOU'RE BETTER than me, don't you?'

Can you believe she said that? My own sister?

I just want to make her see that she can have a better life, you know? If only she would get her act together and get a job, she would feel so much better, I just know it. And, yes, I know it's not that simple for her, but...for goodness sake! Would she rather I left her to rot away in that flat?

Someone at the door... probably another charity collection.

Okay, just some woman who says her car is broken down and she forgot her phone, and can she use mine. Does she think I was born yesterday?

Where was I? Oh yes, the 'Katie Problem.' Door bell again. If it's that woman...

What a night. I really need this coffee! It *was* the same woman again, and this time she was in a right state. Turns out her child had an accident at the park and they were trying to get her to A&E. Well, once I realised they were for real, of course, I sprang into action and drove them there myself.

Would you believe it? Katie was there...not as a patient this time, but with her neighbour – the old lady. Anyway, she'd had a fall. And, somehow, here was Katie the nurse, efficient...in control. Do you know? I'd forgotten all about the old Katie.

Anyway, we spent the night at A&E – on equal terms – monitoring our respective charges. I wanted to make sure the little girl would be okay.

We had a real conversation: I listened and didn't give one single piece of advice. I'm learning... I really need to keep Little Miss Judgemental on a tight leash.

Freedom is a Slippery Thing

'So what is it that you want from these sessions?'

A standard opening gambit. Anne would use this with all her new clients, and I have my answer ready.

'Freedom.'

'Maybe we could unpack that a bit...'

Again, a predictable move...a prompt. But this time my answer isn't ready. The whole thing is too big for one answer. Too big. Like an oversized plate of food that you know you have to eat every morsel of but no idea where to begin or how to tackle the immensity of the challenge ahead. I thought about *Man v Food*, one of my afternoon TV shows.

'Stella?'

I look at her, my mind blank. I've no idea of anything beyond the word 'Freedom'. I've no idea what lies behind that door. Instead I focus on Anna in her baggy jumper and jeggings, her frizzy greying hair, and her blue eyes regarding me through designer rims. I know expensive glasses when I see them.

'You said freedom...' She shifts in the wing-back chair, as if willing me into action of some kind.

'Yes. That's as far as I've got.' It's a stalling move, putting the ball in her court.

'Right. What do you think freedom looks like? For you?'

So freedom is not the same for everyone? That complicates things even further, but I'll have a stab at it – a rough sketch. I lean forward, concentrating. 'Freedom from getting up at six, having breakfast at eight, and getting everything done before my programmes start – I can't miss anything. I'm exhausted and in bed by eight.' The words come out in a rush and I'm amazed at myself for giving such a comprehensive answer. 'That's the kind of thing,' I add, just to make sure that Anna doesn't think these are the only elements of my imprisonment.

Anna hasn't moved a muscle, but now she glances out of the window and back at me. I worry I've disappointed her, that my answer wasn't what she wanted. Suddenly, it's important to have Anna's approval.

'Who says you have to do all these things?'

'No one.' Good, an easy answer. We're back on track again.

'Let me re-phrase. Why do you do all these things?'

'Because otherwise I'll... Everything will spiral out of control and I'll be...' I can't think how to end the sentence. I search my brain, but it comes up with a blank. I look at Anna for clues, but she is impassive, leaning back in the chair, waiting.

I can feel panic mounting. I don't know the answer.

'I don't know,' is all I can manage.

'Okay, let's go back a bit. When did you start to feel that you weren't free?' A sense of failure washes over me. I didn't get it right and now we have to go back and try another tack.

I hide my face in my hands.

'Stella?' I open my eyes and my pulse quickens. Anna is leaning towards me. Suddenly, I matter. She cares.

'It's okay. Sometimes getting started is the hardest bit, Stella.'

Is she being patronising? I give her the benefit of the doubt, and nod. Silence sits between us as I search for something to say.

'How long have you felt like this? Weeks? Months? Longer?'

Multiple choice – I plump for one option. 'Months.'

Anna doesn't respond. All this silence is starting to do my head in. I look away from Anna, out of the window.

'I think that's enough for today.' She sits upright, now business-like and remote. I feel disorientated and notice that an hour has passed. 'Can you come at the same time next week?'

'Yes, yes of course.' Anna is standing, signalling the end of the session – because that's what it is, I remind myself. I'm sure she won't give me a second thought once she's written up her notes.

As I watch *Escape to the Country*, I think about Anna, and it's the same with *Ice-Road Truckers*. I wonder what she is doing, whether she has a family, where she lives, what her friends are like. When I go out for my Tuesday morning shop, I scan the supermarket aisles, hoping to see her, even though the rational side of me knows she won't be there.

As my next appointment approaches, I rehearse what I'm going to say. I'll be better prepared this time. I try to organise my thoughts. I go through my script over and over.

Then I am here again, with Anna, in this capsule where time stands still for an hour.

'How have you been, Stella?' Another classic opening gambit.

'Okay.' But I know it's a lie. I can't tell her that she has been constantly on my mind; somehow, I know she wouldn't like that. It would be stepping over an unspoken boundary.

'So, have you had any thoughts about when you started to feel that you weren't free?'

I've prepared this answer and rehearsed it in my head many times. 'It happened gradually, after I left work.' I stop, waiting for her to respond.

'What was your work?'

'I was an optician.' Your turn, Anna.

'What happened?'

'I started getting panic attacks, sometimes at work, and the patients didn't like it. It scared them. They gave me time off to sort myself out, but somehow...I didn't. I left and my life fell apart, but I put it together again with a timetable for the day. And now, I'm trapped by it.'

'Do you know why you were having these panic attacks?'

This isn't in the script. At this point Anna is supposed to start giving me a road map out of this quagmire. Instead, she's dragging me back into it.

'I don't see what that's got to do with it – I haven't had one in ages.' I'm aware of a huffiness in my voice. I press my knees together and push my heels into the ground. I am not going there.

'Well, it seems to me that it was the panic attacks that got you into this predicament, and it is your timetable that is keeping you safe but imprisoning you at the same time. What do you think? Is that how you see it?' I think that is the longest sentence Anna has spoken. I study her. Today, she is wearing another baggy jumper with blue leggings, and ankle boots – and a different pair of designer glasses. 'Stella?'

I remember she asked a question and turn my gaze to the window. 'Yes... I guess...'

'So, if we can get to grips with where all this started, maybe you'll find a way to get your life back again.' Anna sits back in the chair and crosses her legs. She has good legs, and I wonder why she is proud of her legs but not her body.

'I don't think I can. Isn't there some other way?'

'Not if you want your freedom back.'

'So that's it then? I have to go backwards to be able to get free?'

'If it's easier, why don't you write it all down this week? Then maybe read it out to me next time. People often find it's an easier way to deal with difficult memories.'

It's the day before my next session, and I haven't done my homework. Instead, I've been researching Anna. Her website tells me she has a degree in social work and lots of counselling qualifications. She works with a group of other counsellors in the building I visit every week. I can't find anything else online – no social media, nothing. So I have started to construct a life for Anna: she has a handsome, successful surgeon husband (How else would she afford all those designer frames?), a big house – Edwardian with leaded stained glass in the front door. Three or four children, all successful, maybe the youngest still at uni. I might even give her a grandchild.

In the waiting area, my heart is pounding as I wait for Anna to appear.

And then we are back in our shared cocoon again, and I will my thoughts to stop whirring.

'Did you manage to write anything?'

No, I was too busy thinking about you. For a moment I wonder if I've spoken aloud. 'No, I think it's easier just to talk.' Today, she has contained her wild hair in a scarf – more of a Bohemian vibe. I like it.

And then I tell her everything.

I can't stop talking. I want Anna to know everything. I want her to know me better than anyone else does. The air is filled with the sound of screaming metal on metal, the smell of leaking petrol and the taste of blood in my mouth; the merciful oblivion that wraps me in darkness until I wake up in hospital, a police constable by my side, reassuring me that the child has survived and the parents accept that I couldn't have avoided the collision.

The air between us hangs heavy with grief, horror, guilt and anger. Yes, anger! A self-pitying *Why me?* has emerged from the wreckage. I look out of the window. There is some stability and comfort in the brick wall across the yard.

When I turn back, Anna is leaning towards me, elbows on her knees, hands clasped, and my heart, still doing summersaults from the re-telling, pounds in my chest. I feel myself almost swooning in the heat of her gaze.

'And you've never spoken about all this? For two years?'

'No, you are the only one...' I leave the statement hanging, deliberately vague.

I'm not taken by surprise this time, when she sits back and reaches for her diary. I'm ready for the change of gear. But this time it's more gradual. She sits, looking at the book on her lap for a few seconds. 'I think you have taken a huge step today, Stella. Thank you for sharing with me.'

Uh-oh. More counsellor speak. But I turn a blind eye, choosing to remember the magic moments when her entire attention is focused on me – as if there are no others in that moment except Anna and Stella.

The following week, I continue my research. More extreme measures are called for. Instead of watching my afternoon TV programmes, I break with tradition and park outside the counselling centre. This must mean I am getting better – *Well done, Stella.*

Two hours pass before Anna emerges. In that time I've seen various people come and go, and am consumed with jealous anger at the thought of any of them sharing that special space that belongs to Anna and me. She is wearing a woollen coat and has a leather bag slung over her shoulder. I remember how shocked I was when I saw Miss Gilbert out shopping when I was at primary school – in my head she only existed in the classroom – maybe venturing as far as the playground. I feel a tingle of excitement in my stomach.

I've given her some kind of Volvo in my head, something eco-friendly and Scandinavian. But she approaches a Fiat 500 parked in the corner of the car park next door to the centre. I give her time to get started and then follow at a discreet distance. Anna is a careful driver, indicating well in advance and never exceeding the speed limit. Quite easy to follow. I've missed all my programmes and I couldn't care less. A sense of euphoria is setting in.

She pulls into the drive of a house in a new-build development a few miles outside the city. There is a Nissan Juke already parked in front of the single garage. I pull in and turn my lights off. Anna is getting out of the car and opening the boot. She has two bags of groceries – she must have got them at lunchtime. It's a good job the weather is cold. The front door opens as Anna approaches and another woman is there, wearing some kind of ambulance uniform. She hugs Anna and kisses her. The door is closed and Anna disappears into another world. One that I cannot access. I sit pondering on how wrong I was in the life I had constructed for her.

I drive home slowly, dissecting and examining every detail. On a whim, I stop at a Pizza Hut and sit inside savouring the Deep Crust Marguerita. The clock tells me it is half past seven, and I don't even care. Am I better? Is this what freedom feels like? In one way I feel energised and thrilled that I seemed to have escaped my self-made prison, but another part of me wonders about this newfound liberty. Is this what freedom is like?

We are back in our space, Anna and me. But somehow things are different – the sense of mystery has been diluted. Maybe I know too much. Anna is just another person who gets the shopping at lunchtime.

'How have you been, Stella? I know last time was hard going.'

All I can see is Anna in the arms of the paramedic woman. I can't focus. I don't know why I'm here anymore. I want to say, 'Can we just go and get a coffee?'

We get through the session. I can't remember much about it until it is time to finish.

'I think you've come such a long way, Stella. Do you think you can begin to see a way forward now?'

Wait! Is she suggesting that I might not need many more sessions? I'm not ready to finish – I'm only just getting going. What would my life be without my hour with Anna every week?

I answer carefully. 'I think I've still got quite a journey ahead, but yes, you're right. I've made a start.'

That weekend, I go to Anna and Green Woman's house. It's daylight so I need to be careful. I pull past the house and watch through the rear-view and wing mirrors – all those day-time cop shows have paid off.

After three hours I am thinking of calling it a day and heading back to Pizza Hut when the door opens, and they both come out with a little white dog. I can tell that there is some kind of argument going on – the Green Woman has an aggressive hands-on-hips stance and is leaning forward as she shouts. I open the window and hear the dog barking and growling. Anna puts her hands up in some kind of placating gesture. The Green Woman strides towards me, Anna and the dog following. I hold my breath as they pass the car in silence. Anna running to catch up. She tries to take the Green Woman's arm but is shaken off.

I spend the next few days obsessing about Anna. Should I say something? Should I find out where the Green Woman works and tell her what I know? Who knows what goes on behind closed doors! In the end I do nothing.

The time for our special hour has come round again. I look at Anna and begin to understand the baggy jumpers. Everyone needs something to hide behind. A sense of disappointment and anti-climax is closely followed by anger. I have told Anna things no one else has heard, but at the end of the day she forgets about me and goes home to an abusive partner. (I have convinced myself about this.) She is no better than me. What gives her the right to meddle in my life, when she can't even sort her own out?

I stand. 'I'm done with this. Who do you think you are anyway? Your life is just as much a prison as mine was.' I note the past tense.

'So what kind of life do you envisage that's not a prison?' she says calmly. She doesn't ask how I know about her life.

'One where no one is telling me what to do, and how to live, for a start!'

'But isn't that what you came here to try and escape? Even if that person is yourself?'

Check mate. I seem to have swapped one prison for another. We sit in silence.

'So what does freedom look like? For you.' We are back where we started. Freedom is a slippery thing.

Unwanted Visitors

There had to be a ghost story!

LOTTIE DREW BACK THE curtain and peered outside. The streetlight cast an eerie halo around the street where no one lived but her. Everyone had moved out weeks ago, but Lottie had stood firm, refusing all offers of compensation. She enjoyed being a thorn in the side of the developers – greedy bastards.

But tonight something unfamiliar had woken her. Something different from the usual nocturnal sounds of the drunks and drug dealers who had started to inhabit the vacant street during the hours of darkness. Something... What was it?

She stood for a while, watching the furtive and not-so-furtive comings and goings, amazed at how soon a place could change once no one lived there. They weren't just nocturnal human visitors either. Lottie had seen foxes and bats, and even an owl swooping on an unfortunate rat. Lottie wasn't bothered about any of these new night-time neighbours. She just studied them with an interested curiosity.

Something was different tonight though, and she needed to find out what it was. Lottie turned the bedside light on, slipped her feet into the slip-on sandals she always wore, and headed down the stairs to the front door. She turned the latch and opened it, feeling the cold, clammy autumn air on her skin. Closing the door carefully behind her and pulling her cardigan close under folded arms, Lottie crept, almost invisible in the shadows, along to the corner. There, she stood and waited. If she was going to find out, it would be here. From this corner Lottie could see in five different directions, could see anyone approaching her street. Since the developers had fenced off the far end, the only access to Oak Street was from the Fiveways Roundabout.

Lottie recognised her brother's walk and could hear him dragging the usual stick along the fence, before he came fully into view from her left. The quick intake of breath caught in her throat and Lottie had to battle against the cough threatening to explode from her. She willed herself to stand very still and accept what was coming. She knew from past experience that running got you nowhere.

'Hello, Sis.' Tom, who'd never moved past his tenth birthday, greeted the sixty-five-year-old Lottie as if he'd just got in from school. He threw the stick into the road.

Lottie swallowed and forced herself to answer. 'Hello, Tom.'

'Is that all you've got to say to your long-lost little brother? No hugs? Not even a kiss?' Tom stepped forward, turning his head as if inviting a kiss.

'Come on, Tom. What are you doing here?'

'You look really old, Lottie, and you've shrunk. Look, we're almost the same height now.' Tom laughed the same old giggle. Mirth laced with malevolence.

'Of course I'm old. I'm fifty-five years older than you! What do you want, Tom? Why now?'

'I had to come back home to see Oak Street and our old house one more time before it's all knocked down. It will be, you know that, don't you? Even though you've fought them, you won't be able to stop it.' There was a pause as Tom adjusted the belt on his gaberdine raincoat and pulled his school cap forward as if to shield his eyes. 'Well come on, then, what are we waiting for? I can't wait to get home.'

Lottie felt his hand on her arm, guiding her firmly and inevitably back along the street.

Once they were in the kitchen, Tom sat in his usual place at the table. 'I knew you wouldn't have changed anything – you wouldn't have dared, would you? I'm starving. How about some beans on toast? That's what you usually make me when I get home from school.'

'You can't eat anything, Tom. You're a ghost.'

'I know, but I still want to watch you making it. In our kitchen – just one more time.'

Lottie obeyed and put some bread in the toaster. Anything to have something to do. Anything to avoid going upstairs with Tom.

The smell of toast and the heated baked beans on the plate in front of Tom hung, cloying, in the air. 'I really enjoyed that. Thanks, Sis.' Tom leant back in the chair smacking his lips. Lottie shuddered at their greyish-blue pallor. 'I know. Death doesn't look good, does it, Lottie?'

He pushed the chair back, scraping it noisily along the floor as he stood. 'Right-ho. Let's have a look upstairs. Shall we start with your room? I'm guessing you're in Mum and Dad's old room, now. You always did like to have a window facing the front.'

Lottie, now feeling strangely calm, almost glad that the moment had come, stood and strode rapidly into the hall. 'Come on, then, slow coach!' She turned and spoke over her shoulder. They mounted the stairs and Lottie was aware of Tom behind her, strangely silent. There were none of the familiar creaks. She felt goosebumps across her arms.

'This is my room.' Everything was as she'd left it – the bedside light on and the covers flung back. 'I wonder what Mum and Dad think of you sleeping in their old bed? Don't you think it's a bit creepy, Sis?'

Lottie didn't answer, returning to the landing and closing the door firmly behind her as if Tom hadn't been there. Nevertheless he reappeared at her side.

'No need to be like that!' Still just as moody as ever.

Lottie sighed. 'Right, let's get this over with, shall we?' She led the way to Tom's room and opened the door.

'Where are all my things?'

'Tom, you've been dead for fifty-five years!'

'You shouldn't have got rid of my things.' There was a note of menace in his voice now and Lottie felt a tingle of unease creep across her scalp. Meetings with Tom had never gone well on the few occasions he had visited since his death. They had lived on in Lottie's nightmares for months and years afterwards. But he had never wanted to come into the house before; he'd always found her on the street or in the park on one of her insomnia-fuelled walks. This time things were different, and Lottie had no idea how she would recover from Tom's presence in the house.

'You shouldn't have got rid of my things!' Lottie closed her eyes but could feel his deathly cold presence on her face as he came close to her. 'You took my life and now you've taken my things.'

'What good were they to you when you weren't even here anymore?' As the words left her mouth, Lottie knew she'd said the wrong thing and sat on the stripped bed as her legs trembled and gave way.

'You bitch! What did I ever do to deserve a sister like you?' The words came in an icy hiss and Lottie felt her blood run cold. 'What other boy had a sister

who smothered him with a pillow? In...his...own.
..bed.' Tom poked her arm with his index finger,
emphasising each word, and she flinched each time
even though she could feel nothing through her
cardigan.

At this humiliation, anger returned to Lottie. The
anger from all those years ago. 'I hated you then,
and I hate you now! You monster! You made my
life a misery with your sly stories to Mum and Dad
and my friends, and your little "pranks." I had to
check my bed every night for creepy-crawlies or
God-knows-what before I could sleep.'

'What a laugh! You never could take a joke, Sis. But
maybe now it's time to even the score.'

She stared at the door, knowing there was no escape.

'You shouldn't have done that to your brother,
Charlotte.' She heard her father's voice. 'Look at me
when I'm talking to you!' Lottie turned back to look
at Tom.

'You are a bad girl to do something like that to
Tom, so you'll have to be punished.' This time her
mother's admonishing voice erupted from Tom's
mouth, his expression mirroring her mother's familiar expression of displeasure.

Lottie, powerless against the force of her family,
curled herself into a ball on the bed as if she, like
them, could disappear. But of course, she couldn't.
She didn't have that power yet.

'It's okay, Miss Crawford. We're here now. Don't worry about a thing.' Lottie opened her eyes to meet those of the green-clad paramedic who was holding her hand. 'Where...? What...?' She seemed to have lost the power of speech.

'You've had a bit of a turn, so we're just going to pop you to hospital to get you checked out.'

Lottie closed her eyes, trying to focus her thoughts. 'How...?'

'How did we know to come? Your brother rang to say he was worried that you didn't sound yourself when he was on the phone. He thought you might have lost consciousness when you stopped speaking.'

'My brother...?'

'Your brother, Tom.'

Originally published on *https://greythoughts.info/t hewritersclub* 20 November 2021

Christmas Ice

THE DETAILS ON THE fir trees were finished and Sam
sat back to study her work. She knew she could
always do more but had learnt over the years when
enough was enough. Leaning back in her chair and
stretching her arms above her head, she noticed the
robin, perched in his usual place on the back of the
bench in the garden. He tilted his head, looking at
her solemnly through the glass.

This piece was special which made the pressure to
achieve perfection even greater. It was her father's
Christmas present and she'd been working on it all
through November. Mirroring the robin, she tilted her head and examined the painting again. The
winter sun on the water was just right, reflected in
a rosy blush on the mountain peaks in the distance.
Just a few stray snowflakes maybe? No, let the light
be the main focus. Her photographer father would
appreciate that, she hoped.

Leaving the canvas to dry, Sam made a cup of
coffee and, putting on her puffa jacket, went to sit on

the bench outside – the robin having disappeared as suddenly as it had arrived. Blowing on the steam rising into the cold air Sam clasped her hands around the mug for warmth. She was fighting a battle for her father's love and attention, and her adversary was Diane, apparently her soon-to-be stepmother. Sam considered Diane – a talented singer and musician (her father always went for arty types), and, most worryingly, still young enough to have a child. After her mother's death when she was six, Sam and her father had been a tight unit – clinging to one another for survival through their shared memories of Lisa. Yes, he had had 'girlfriends,' Sam was realistic enough to know that would happen, but Diane was different. The look in his eyes when he introduced her over dinner had told Sam everything – he looked at Diane with a look that had always been hers until now. He even called her the same names – Sweetie; Hun; Princess (yes really!) In the past Sam had cringed at the last one, but now that someone else was claiming ownership of it, it was suddenly worth more than gold.

A few days after the introduction, over a coffee–and-cake debrief at the café around the corner, her father had asked, 'Well?'

'Well what?' Sam had been unable to hide her panic.

'Oh, Sam...'

'Don't patronise me, Dad. You go live your life. Look at me, I'm all grown up now. I can look out for myself. You get on and live your life.' Sam hated the self-pitying, needy feeling inside, but was unable to stop it from having a voice.

'Maybe if you got to know Diane better—'

'Don't...just don't suggest a girly shopping trip!' Sam held a stop hand in front of her.

She'd felt his sigh, but, unable to stop the force of emotion threatening to overwhelm her, Sam had fled from the shop.

As she strode up the drive on Christmas Day, Sam felt a tingling excitement at the thought of her picture holding pride of place. Maybe in the hall? Or above the fire? She'd had it wrapped and delivered a week ago – plenty of time to get it hung, she figured. The *Thanks for the present xx* text confirmed that it had been received. Sam had been taken aback by the lack of effusiveness in the message at first, but having thought about it, she'd come to the conclusion that her father was saving all the praise for Christmas Day – not wanting to even try to express his feelings in a text. Confident that her reasoning was correct, Sam knocked on the door full of anticipation.

'Happy Christmas, Angel.' The hug was warm and Sam felt safe. (Although, 'Angel' was new)

'Happy Christmas, Dad… Diane.' She nodded a greeting at her adversary hovering at the bottom of the stairs.

'Let's take your coat, and it must be about time for some Christmas mulled wine.'

Glancing around the hallway, Sam could see no sign of her painting – maybe in the lounge then? A roaring fire greeted her as she approached the Christmas tree.

'What do you think?' Diane and I thought we'd start some new traditions, so we've got a new look this year.

'What about all our old decorations? The ones we always have?'

'Well maybe you would like to have them, for when you have your own tree, and maybe your own family.'

'Dad—'

'Sam, this is how it is. I'm sorry if it's hard for you.' There was that impatience in his voice again. That unheard sigh.

And no painting. Maybe the kitchen?

'I'll just go and see if Diane needs any help – I know where everything is.' She followed the sound of clattering saucepan lids and running water.

'Sam.'

'Hi Diane. Anything I can do?'

'No thanks.' The reply was ice cold.

Still no picture.

'Looking for your picture?'

'Well, yes, actually.'

'It's in the upstairs spare room for now. Until I've moved my stuff in, it's difficult to know where to put such a...large painting.'

Sam felt the breath leave her body and she clung onto the back of a chair for support. She detected a sneery tone of triumph. Yes, it *was* a large canvas. She'd wanted to make a statement.

'You okay, Sam?' Diane was all concern now. 'Bob, I don't think Sam is feeling too good.'

Her father rushed into the room, putting his arm around her. 'What is it, Princess?' Okay, 'Princess' was back: a good sign.

'I'm getting a migraine. I don't feel well.'

'Okay, I'll take you home.'

'Thanks, Dad. Would you mind? Sorry, Diane. I'll try not to keep him too long.'

This skirmish had been a draw, but the war was far from over.

Over the following months, Covid made any personal contact difficult and Sam put up a wall of silence following the disaster of Christmas Day.

After a heated argument her father had left Sam's flat, exasperated, slamming the door behind him. He had changed – Diane had changed him – and was now distant, and irritable with her neediness.

Her old father had always understood how Sam had felt – she could have told him anything – but to this new father, she was an irritating nuisance. Everyone's Christmas had been ruined.

Since then, texts, calls and emails from her father remained unread and unanswered. Eventually, they stopped coming altogether and the rift was established while Sam regrouped and planned her next move. Sam hated the person she had become – vengeful and angry – but found a strange comfort in being that person. More than anything, she wanted to destroy Diane and punish her father, even if it meant causing herself pain in the process.

But everything changed when she met Dan. Over the summer holidays romance blossomed as they spent long, languid days and nights away from the stress and pressures of college, and teaching under Covid restrictions. Sam had been drawn to him immediately when he joined the staff at the beginning of the summer term. As they got to know each other over coffees and long walks, she could feel her icy anger and bitterness beginning to thaw under his kindness and good humour. One night, she had told him everything about last Christmas and he had held her, tears in his eyes. 'I'm so sorry, Sam, it must have been awful. How unkind and cruel. Maybe it's better to let them go their own way if they're going to treat you like that.'

'But that's not who my father is. He's changed.'

'The people we meet often change us as we fall under their spell, and not always for the better. There's nothing you can do, Sam, and you're not a bad person for keeping your distance and keeping yourself safe. Think of it like your father is under a spell. You can't do anything until he wakes up.'

'You think?' Sam sat up and looked into his eyes.

'Yes, I do think.' He jumped up. 'You need a distraction. I know, let's get the train to Cambridge and go punting.'

Sam loved his spontaneity and sense of fun. Over the months Dan filled her mind and her life until there was little room for her father and Diane. The war seemed petty, on reflection.

The first time Sam met Dan's mother, she wished she had been her own mother instead of the ghostly memories she had made do with. There was a warmth in the house and Sam had immediately felt at home. Like her, Dan had lost a parent in childhood, but unlike her, he still had the remaining one. Sam found herself spending more time with Dan at Mia's house and eventually started visiting on her own when Dan was busy. Mia was an amazing cook and taught Sam all the basic skills, right from boiling an egg. They spent many happy Saturdays in Mia's kitchen.

While they were having a cup of tea and waiting for the bread dough to rise one afternoon, Mia said, 'Why don't you invite your father over?'

Sam immediately froze, the cup halfway between the saucer and her mouth. 'What?'

'I know you're not in touch, and I can only imagine how painful it is for you. Why don't you message him and see how he is? Even if you do it for yourself.'

'No way.'

'Sam, eight months have gone by. Things may have changed for him, as they have for you. Why not find out how things stand? Give him a chance.'

Sam pondered when she got home. She thought about how her feelings for Dan had blossomed and understood how her father might have felt the same way about Diane. Her finger hovered over the buttons on her phone. Eventually, after a large gulp of red wine she messaged, pressing Send before she had time to overthink:

> *Hi Dad. I was just wondering how you are.*
> *Sam*

An immediate reply bounced onto the screen:

> *Sam, how lovely to hear from you. I've missed you so much. Xx*

Without thinking, Sam typed a reply:

Can we meet for coffee?

Yes. Usual place? Are you free tomorrow morning?

Yes, okay. See you at 11 x

Once they were seated at their usual table, her father reached over and took Sam's hand. There was a long silence as they looked into each other's eyes.

'Sam, I'm so sorry about last Christmas; we were nasty and cruel to you. I don't know what I was thinking.' He squeezed her hand. 'I absolutely love your painting and I can guess how much work went into it. Can you forgive me?'

Sam drew her hand away and looked down at the table. 'What about Diane?'

'Well, things are complicated.' He sighed. 'I have realised that she is not the person I want to share my life with. I can't forgive her for the way we treated you – I know it's not just her fault – I allowed it to happen. It's like I was under some kind of spell.'

Sam waited.

'Anyway, I've asked her to move out but she's refusing, so it may come to taking legal action. Things are very tense.'

Suddenly the ice melted as Sam's eyes filled with tears. 'Oh, Dad...' She squeezed his hand. 'I'm so glad I've got you back.'

Preparations for Christmas were well underway, even though Covid restrictions seemed to be changing by the day. Sam had spent time with her father repairing and healing the wounds of battle. Diane, when threatened with lawyers had reluctantly and angrily moved out.

As promised, Mia had invited them all round for Sunday lunch a few times, and Sam had a sneaking feeling that her father may have received some invitations that she and Dan hadn't been privy to. In return, Sam's father had insisted they all come to his house for Christmas Day, as long as Mia was in charge of the cooking, ably assisted by Sam.

As Sam and Dan walked up the drive on Christmas morning, she reflected on how things could have turned out so differently. What if the anger and bitterness had kept growing? What if she hadn't met Dan...and Mia?

'You seem miles away, Sam.' Dan put his arm around her and held her close. 'It's going to be different this year. You know that don't you?' It was almost as if he could read her thoughts.

Her father flung open the door and enveloped Sam in a tight, safe, bear hug. He gave Dan the same warm reception. 'Happy Christmas, Princess.'

'Oh, for God's sake, Dad. I'm not six!' Sam felt a warm glow inside. There was no room for ice now.

'Well, what are you waiting for? Get those coats off and let's get stuck in to coffee and mince pies.'

As if on cue, Mia appeared with a plate of goodies. 'Could you get the coffee pot, Bob?' Sam noted the familiar tone and smiled to herself.

As she entered the room, Sam stopped breathing. There was her picture, in pride of place over the roaring fire. 'Ohhh.' She could feel self-control slipping away as a sob escaped her.

'Oh Sam. That is something else! You're wasted at the college.' Dan's eyes shone with admiration.

She rushed, childlike, across the room to the Christmas tree. 'Ohhh, they're all here!' Her father put his arm around her, pulling her close. He smelt like Dad again.

'These are all our Christmas memories,' he said to Dan and Mia, indicating the decorations on the tree – all except last Christmas, which we shall erase. As they exchanged presents, enjoying the coffee and mince pies, Sam spied the robin perched on a branch near the window. He tilted his head to one side. They gazed at each other for a few seconds before he flew off.

Originally published on https://cafelit.co.uk/ 8 December 2021

If you enjoyed Shifting Horizons...

It would make my day if you could just take a few minutes to pop over to the Shifting Horizons Amazon page and leave a review or if Goodreads is your thing, a review over there would be equally welcome.

From Manchester to the Arctic, Sheena's full-length novel, is now available

Set in the Hudson Bay area of Arctic Canada in the 1970s, *From Manchester to the Arctic* recalls a way of life that no longer exists, and the challenges that it brought for a girl from Manchester who didn't know what she was letting herself in for, or who she was.

"A hope filled and immersive coming of age story about a nurse on an incredible journey." Love Reading

"What a breath of fresh air! This book is so many books encompassed into one, which I really loved. Drama, romance, adventure, and tension all in one! I came to love the community that Connie found herself in, the people she interacted with, and the relationships that built." Book Sirens

"Go on a journey to the Arctic with Connie in this novel. From Manchester to the Arctic is a well-written story depicting the lives and challenges of members of a small community in the Arctic. I loved the characters and their diverse personalities." Reader's Favorite

Available on all Amazon platforms

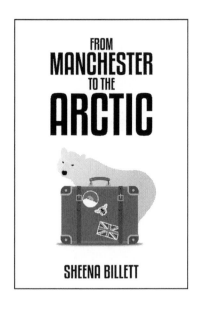

Keep in Touch

If you would like updates about my writing and sneek previews of up and coming books head over to https://sheenabillettauthor.com and sign up for my newsletter.

Vanstone Press

Printed in Great Britain
by Amazon

17566232R00130